The Sacred River

Gitura Kihuria

Nsemia

First Edition September 2012

Edited by Charles Phebih-Agyekum
Cover Concept & Design: Gitura Kihuria
Cover Layout Design: Danielle Pitt

Published by Nsemia Inc. Publishers
Oakville, Ontario, Canada
www.nsemia.com

Note for Librarians:
A cataloguing record for this book is available
from Library and Archives Canada

ISBN: 978-1-926906-23-2 paperback

What happens to a dream deferred?
Does it dry up like a raisin in the sun?
Or fester like a sore – and then run.
- Langstone Hughes (1902-1967)

American Writer, Essayist & Poet

TABLE OF CONTENTS

This book is dedicated to the memory of all the people who fought and struggled for freedom in pre and post-colonial Kenya
To my parents Mr. & Mrs. Kihuria, and my siblings Mukora, Githinji and Wanjihia
And to Mohamed Bouazizi who triggered the Arab Spring Revolution by self immolation

ACKNOWLEDGEMENTS

It is with sincere gratitude and heartfelt pleasure that I acknowledge and thank my parents for their love and providence. They struggled to put us in school and gave us the best inheritance a parent can give their child, education.

Dad, I extol your virtues and spirit which remains unbowed through your health nightmare. Your stoicism and dignity with which you brave the horrifying reality of having to stay in a body ravaged by a chronic illness.

I am thankful to my dear wife and soul mate, Bertha for believing in me.

I am indebted to my editor Charles Phebih-Agyekum for his the very useful advice and dedication to make this book a reality.

ABOUT THE AUTHOR

Gitura Kihuria was born and raised in Nairobi. Together with his three brothers he would be hauled by their parents to *ushago* (up-country) to visit their grandparents during school holidays, in line with the trend back then. Here, he first encountered the scenic and picture-postcard beauty of the Kenyan countryside.

Gitura went to Harambee Primary School and later joined Dagoretti High School (Ditchez) before attending KCA University where he studied accounts. He later trained and qualified as a financial consultant. Thereafter he worked in a law firm and an investment company, among others.

He admits that to having an addiction of reading books, a bug he caught while in upper primary school. Here, he lavishly "feasted" on such pop lit' like *Hardyboys* and Ludlam, among others, a trend he continued through high school. His favourite authors here were Fredrick Forsythe, Sidney Sheldon, and Wilbur Smith. Later he would discover African literature through Elechi Amadi's *The Concubine*, which was his literature set book.

It was like epiphany, he says and leading to new worlds of African writers like Chinua Achebe, Ngugi wa Thiongo, Camara Laye, Elechi Amadi, among other African writers.

Today he enjoys reading autobiographies and contemporary writers like Chimamanda Ngozi Adichie of the *Half of a Yellow Sun* fame.

Gitura writes the occasional comment on social issues and good governance in Kenya's leading newspapers namely, the *Nation* and the *East African Standard*. He was an early proponent of the new constitution that Kenyans adopted in 2010. He also blogs on the net and contributes with *Storymoja*.

Definitions

- The president's name, Sonkoh, is derived from a *sheng* (local slang used by the youth in Kenya) word *Sonko*. The word describes a suddenly wealthy person who cannot account for the source of their wealth.

- *Sonkoist* are insecure and fiercely protective of their turf. They act brave, but the bravery is a masquerade. They perspire with rage outside, while trembling with fear inside.

- *Donyokeri*, the name of the country, is derived from the Maasai name of Mt. Kenya, Ol Donyo Keri.

PART ONE

Mid-Sixties

Chapter One

Waciuri was said to have been born with a spring in his gait. He walked with his heels slightly lifted from the ground, like someone always late for an appointment.

For all intents and purposes, Waciuri had an appointment with destiny.

Having been born of a single mother who died while birthing him, Waciuri was brought up by his maternal grandmother whom he considered as his own mother for she filled the yawning gap of the mother figure that he craved.

Njeri, Waciuri's grandmother, for that was her name, had taken over the role of bringing up Waciuri after his mother's (Njeri's daughter) death.

She weaned Waciuri on goat milk, plantain and arrowroots and within no time, he became a strong and sturdy lad, like his grandfather.

If you wanted to meet with Waciuri's grandfather, it was said that it was easier to meet with him at Mutituini town where he always went to imbibe the local brew and the political developments in his country.

Growing up in such circumstances, Waciuri grew a thick skin and a strong personality if only to prove himself.

He would lead his age mates for deer hunting trips into Mutituini forest with a pack of hunting dogs that prodded them to take flight from their hideouts in the undergrowth and run towards the traps they had set along the usual tracks that the deer used.

He was also skilled in setting up mole-traps, which would come in handy when his grandmother planted potatoes in her small farm.

His mole-traps were so effective such that his grandmother's farm was the most productive in terms of output, even though it was much smaller than other farms in the village.

These skills were acquired from the older boys who had now stopped such 'boyish' pastimes after being initiated into adulthood through circumcision.

Sometimes a stray antelope would wander into a nearby ranch owned by Bwana Kamangu but Waciuri and his team would not dare to chase the antelope because of the fierce pitbulls and dobermans that guarded the gated ranch.

In any case, their hunting mongrels were no match for these dogs that were separated by the massive sturdy gate that had *Mbwa kali* (fierce dogs).

They would only wait and listen as the howling dogs made a meal from the unlucky antelope that had dared disturb their peace

The owner of the ranch, Bwana Kamangu, had served the oppressive colonial government in stemming dissent from the peasantry. He was rewarded with a ranch by a *Mzungu* (white) large scale farmer and cattle keeper who left Donyokeri after it gained *uhuru*.

After paying a token to the departing Mzungu, Bwana Kamangu ensured that the farm was a no-go zone for the locals unless you worked in the ranch as a labourer.

***

Donyokeri was a young nation with high expectations.

After the oppressive colonial government had given in to the demands of self-rule, the brave freedom fighter Charles Sonkoh, who led the bush fighters in an armed struggle against Her Majesty's government, promised to unite all the tribes of Donyokeri and start a new page of peace and prosperity.

His political party, Donyokeri Democratic Party-DDP, had won most of the parliamentary seats in the country after the colonial government set in place an electoral process for the natives to choose the party that would represent them in the next government.

At Uhuru Square, a million people from all walks of life gathered to witness as the Union Jack went down and as the brand new flag of a red lion face on a green background went up.

On the dais, the president of the new republic, Charles Sonkoh, received a large hardcover green tome that contained the constitution of the country and other instruments of power from the outgoing governor amid jubilations from the huge crowd.

He raised the constitution towards the crowd and, with his booming and charismatic voice, asked "were we given Uhuru on a silver platter or did we fight for it?"

The crowd replied in unison "we fought for it!"

"I asked! Were we given or did we grab it?" he egged the crowd on.

"We grabbed it!" the crowd shot back in jubilation. The euphoria was palpable, and what a joyous occasion it was.

The president then called for national unity among the tribes that had been torn against each other through the divide-and-rule tactics that the colonial administration had employed to enable a minority lord over the peasantry.

He also called for the citizens to forgive and reach out to the settlers in order to move forward with the business of nation building.

Among the crowd at Uhuru Square was Shujaa Juma from Siala.

He was a recent graduate from Kings Teachers College and had received his letter of appointment as a school principal for Jamhuri Secondary School .The post was left vacant after the former principal left for his country when all signs pointed to Donyokeri gaining independence.

Kings Teachers College based in Rukuna, the capital city of Donyokeri was a walking distance to Uhuru Square and he could not for his life miss the lifetime opportunity of witnessing his country attain self-rule and at last be able to chart its own future.

The country had its own share of challenges, like not having an educated lot like himself.

In fact, college graduates like him were few and scattered in the country.

But with the eloquence that the new president addressed the crowd, no one would doubt the ability of the new country to forge forward.

It was the proudest moment of Juma's life and his eyes glinted with emotions as the national anthem was played.

Chapter Two

Meanwhile in Mutituini village, just like the rest of the country, excitement was in the air as locals celebrated the new found independence.

It was now upon them to chart their future and stop living like second-hand citizens in their forefathers' land.

Locals had gathered at the market place to follow the Independence Day celebrations.

You could see clusters of people gathered at various points where the few villagers who owned transistor radios had tuned in to listen to the Independence Day proceedings.

Business at the market had virtually come to a standstill as everyone animatedly discussed the new development.

Being a market day, the place should have been a bee-hive of activity as locals bartered whatever they had brought to the market. But today, locals were glued to the few transistor radios that were around.

Those who owned them were highly regarded as they were seen to be wealthy in those days.

And what a better day than this auspicious occasion to flaunt their wealth.

In fact, the young industrious men who owned them would invite the village damsels they fancied over to their abodes and ensure that the radios were tuned to the *BBC* channel.

Even though none of them understood the English programmes that were broadcast from the radios, they left a lasting impression on the young women.

Obviously, the young men who owned them were the envy of the village.

Waciuri and his age mates had also gone to the market but for different reasons.

They had gone to the market to sell and barter the guinea fowls they had trapped. But it was not the best of days for them because no one was trading.

Left with nothing useful to engage themselves in, they devised games and pranks which they played among themselves.

Such games would include tying one leg of the guinea fowls that they had caught with a string that was secured to the ground by a wooden peg and egging the cocks to fight each other.

And the birds would not disappoint as they fought each other out of frustration and hunger.

Another game devised by their counterparts, - the girls would involve tying strings on yellow and black spotted beetles. Once the beetles flapped their wings to fly off, they would grab the strings like one would a kite and see which beetle would last longer in the air.

The day was coming to a close in Mutituini' market and no one seemed to be in a hurry to head back to their homes.

The smouldering orb was now dropping and going to slumber as it dutifully did every day, just like mothers would tell their children in the evening when reminding them to take the livestock into their enclosures. It left an iridescent orange-yellow glow on the horizon and on the clouds above.

Gradually, darkness settled in the market and the villagers decided to light bonfires to celebrate the ending day.

The mood was carnival and they danced the night off as young men beat the drums rhythmically while young women gyrated their hips wrapped in *lessos* (wrappers) and the old folks reminisced about the good old days when rare occasions called for such celebrations.

***

Jamhuri Secondary School located in Mutituini village was a day's drive from Rukuna the capital city of Donyokeri.

Juma, who had packed a few personal belongings in his suitcase, was headed to the bus on his way to the new posting.

He boarded one of the old yellow buses christened *Msamaria Mwema* (Good Samaritan) that plied the route at the bus terminus. The shape of the bus reminded him of Elliott's bread with its curved front and backside. Finally, the driver, chewing one end of a toothpick, sauntered into the driver's cabin after keeping the passengers waiting impatiently for him.

After it coughed and spattered to life, the driver drove to the local petrol station to fill the tank and balance the tyre pressure, leaving everyone wondering why he didn't have the common sense to take care of such obvious tasks before driving the vehicle to the stage.

Speed was not one of its strengths and it spewed black diesel smoke as it clambered up steep roads.

It was going to be a long day for Juma and he opted to make good use of the long hours by going through the syllabus that was handed to him by the provincial education officer from the Ministry of Education.

But as he soon found out, the bus would not provide the quiet environment he so much craved to enable him go through the syllabus.

The bus had all sorts of travelling passengers including livestock such as sheep, goats, chicken, et cetera, which occupied the middle row of the seats.

The sheep would bleat while the chickens clucked, producing a cacophony of sounds.

The heavy-set middle-aged woman seated beside

him with a suckling baby did not make matters easier.

The baby would tug his collar when is mother held him up on her bosom to make him burp and Juma resigned himself to his fate and started making funny faces at the baby when his mother was not looking. This would earn him a toothless grin from the baby.

Chapter Three

One week after independence, the president decreed that all children up to primary level who attended public school should not pay school fees to ensure that those who were unable to pay did not miss out.

This was one of the plans in the ruling party's manifesto that was meant to eradicate illiteracy in the young nation.

The future of Donyokeri looked bright with such road side declarations from the president.

***

Juma liked the school the first time he set his eyes on it. It was the best school in the village.

It had two streams for each class, a big school in that part of the country.

It was surrounded by a hedge fence of a spiny evergreen shrub that produced yellow tangy fruits during certain seasons. The fruits were superstitiously thought to be snake fruits, by children in the village.

The principal's house was at the far end of the school compound and had a bougainvillea fence around it, which offered some degree of privacy.

The students had also received him warmly, especially the girls because of his youthful athletic looks.

He grew his hair long to an afro and unkept look, which gave him a rugged sexy look.

The other reason they liked him was because of his clear, sliding English, unlike the nasal English the former white principal spoke, which they found hard to comprehend.

However, other teachers, especially the older ones who had served long in the school, felt envious of him but they had to contend with the fact that he was the most learned of them all.

Apart from being the principal, he also taught English and Geography in the senior classes, eliciting a lot of excitement from female students.

***

Waciuri, who had enrolled for primary school as was required by the government was busy helping his grandmother cook the evening meal by fanning the dying embers.

"What did you learn in school today?" his grandmother prodded as she put the dried smoked strips of meat in the frothing stew in the pot.

"The teacher taught us to recite the song London Bridge is Falling Down," Waciuri replied while coughing from the smoke that was filling the kitchen as he was fanning the embers.

In school they were taught how to read and write in English, basic math and Bible study.

His eyes had become teary from the smoke that had engulfed the kitchen and his young wrist was now aching from the constant fanning.

Finally, the embers ignited with a whoosh sound and then the fire started burning briskly with a crackling sound.

The stew in the pot was now boiling at a steady pace and the room was now less smoky.

"*Cucu* (grandmother), but I don't like the songs and the stories that we are taught at school," Waciuri said.

"I don't understand them and they are not like the proverbs and fables you tell me in the evenings," he added.

"You have to learn *githungu* (English) if you want to succeed in the future," Waciuri's grandmother admonished. "If you want to be someone big in the government, you have to learn *githungu*," she emphasized.

With that, Waciuri was only left in his own thoughts as he reminisced about some of the stories that his grandmother would regularly narrate.

He smiled, especially when he remembered the one of the greedy hyena.

The story goes as follows: - "Once upon a time, the hyena went out in search of food.

He wandered wide; - through the valleys and hills, when at last he saw a calf tied to a pole near the village.

He raised his ears with pleasure and began to boast saying, - 'thou sayeth, Lord, it is thou who provideth me with food, snatch away from me if you can, this calf which I have found for myself!'

Meanwhile it came near the calf thinking, 'what shall I begin with? Do I begin with the leather rope or with the calf?'

He decided to begin with the rope, reserving the tender flesh of the calf for the end. But as it was munching at the rope, the calf bolted away.

'Oh! Oh! cried out the hyena, Lord God, our Father, it is thou who provideth us with food; - let the calf come back to me.'

It pursued the calf, but with its short hind legs, it was all in vain and he went home hungry."

Chapter Four

Mumbi, Bwana Kamangu's only daughter, was the prettiest girl in the village. She had taken after her mother.

She was of average height and light skinned. She had cropped black hair which glistened when she applied coconut hair oil.

She had brown bewitching eyes and full lips and you could not help but notice the natural gap between her milk-white teeth when she talked as well as her contagious smile.

You would also notice her dimples coming out when she opened her mouth to talk.

Her round breasts stood out firm and defiant like the twin hills of Aberdare Mountains, Elephant Hills and Table Mountains.

And despite her age, eighteen years, she had a full figure. However, her father would not let her interact freely with the "good-for-nothing village brats," as he used to call the many young men in the village.

In fact, the only time Mumbi was to be seen in the village was when she went to school and when they would drive to the market with her father to buy rations, which was not very often. She was now in the final semester before she cleared high school.

Despite her father's aloofness and proud attitude, she was liked by the villagers because she was kind, friendly and pleasant to be around.

Today was one of those rare occasions on which she drove to the market with her father.

He sped as usual along in the former owner's Chevrolet pickup that he inherited together with the ranch, leaving a mushroom cloud of red dust behind.

But Mumbi was deep in her own thoughts in spite of her father's speeding.

Since Principal Juma came to her school, she was always thinking about him.

He was tall and handsome, with broad shoulders and walked with a confident gait.

Unlike other girls in her school who boasted of boyfriends, she had none thanks to her father's vigilance.

She was therefore naïve in such matters but for some strange reasons, her heart would race every time Principal Juma walked into their class to teach geography.

Fortunately, she hoped that he did not notice her infatuation because most girls could not even hide the fact that they had a crush on him.

She was snapped from her reverie and brought back to the world when the car suddenly screeched to a halt.

Bwana Kamangu came out of the car and headed straight to an agrovet owned by an Indian.

"Namaste! Vana Kamangu," Patel greeted with a heavy Indian accent while wobbling his head.

"Vow is your farm doing and vow is your animals?" he enquired.

"Not bad! I just came for some de-worming drugs and pesticides. It has been a while since I took the cattle to the cattle-dip."

***

It had been three months since Juma came to the school and was not distracted by the attention that he attracted from the students.

He was more focused in turning the young impressionable minds in his school into an educated lot that would be able to serve the new nation.

He was particularly fond of a final year student, Mumbi, who carried herself with such dignity and decorum.

She was reserved and not excitable like the other girls in her school, which gave the impression that she was more mature than the rest.

And for that reason, he chose her as the deputy captain of the school. The captain was a boy who led in both athletics and academics.

She would represent the students by bringing students affairs to his attention. She was therefore an important link between the students' and the school administration.

Her visit to his office was thus regular when she came to bring students' issues to his attention. From their interactions, they cultivated a mutual friendship.

Chapter Five

President Sonkoh's leadership, which had heralded a new beginning for the young nation, was starting to waver.

Government appointments were no longer through merit but rather through nepotism and coming from the "correct tribe." In fact, key government jobs in the ministries were headed by his cronies.

Land that had been repossessed from the colonizers to settle the many natives who had been dispossessed of their land was sold fraudulently to well connected individuals who later subdivided them into small parcels and sold them to the highest bidder on a first come basis, making huge profits for themselves.

And his war veteran friends were rewarded with top positions in the police and military.

The turn of events only two years in his leadership started creating a quiet dissent throughout the country, and people would discuss this sad outcome in places like *barazas* (public forums).This was also becoming a topical issue in drinking joints. It was soon picked up by the media.

The media pushed for reforms by urging the government to live up to its promises and not steal the dream of the people, that of a healthy, learned and prosperous nation.

The people of Donyokeri had driven the white man from the country of their forefathers because of his injustices only to have one of their own perpetrate the same things that they had fought against.

It seemed they had driven out the white master only to be replaced by a black one. That was even worse because he was one of their own.

***

It had been three years now since Waciuri started primary school and he had proven to be an outstanding student.

In those days, they did not have exercise books, but they had slates that were painted black and they would use chalk to write down what they were learning during class. The following day, they would wipe their "small blackboards" to be able to write on them again.

Therefore, it was important to have a good memory to remember what had been taught previously.

What made Waciuri outstanding was his photographic memory, which made him recall most of the things that they learnt in school.

They normally carried the black slates and chalk in small leather pouches, that they made from pieces of cattle hide. It was cured by tying the hide with wooden pegs on the ground after scrapping off any leftover pieces of flesh to dry out in the sun.

That was the "school bag" that Waciuri was carrying on his way home when he met Mumbi, who had since finished high school and was waiting to enter college in the capital city.

"How are you doing, young man" she greeted Waciuri as she often did in their local dialect.

She had grown close to Waciuri after his mother's death. She had known her as she used to be a farm hand in her father's ranch.

She would often keep tabs on him now that his grandmother took the full responsibility of bringing him up on her own.

"I'm very well, I have just come from school and I'm heading home," he replied in English so as to make an impression on her. He considered her as the big sister that he never had.

"Say hallo to *cucu* for me and make a point of visiting me one of these days. I'll give you a bag of maize flour to take to your grandmother," she replied.

"I will," Waciuri replied, bade her farewell and they both proceeded with their own separate journeys.

Chapter Six

In the last three years, Juma's indifference towards the new leadership was beginning to show. Apart from teaching his students on good governance and equitable distribution of national resources, he shared his thoughts whenever a *baraza* was convened to discuss the gradual misrule of the country.

And this apathy that people had towards Sonkoh's government did not escape the president's coterie.

They were made up of an inner circle of his kitchen cabinet, who would advise him on how to govern. The business elite from his tribe also wanted favours like government tenders to advance their business empire.

This cabal had direct access to State House or they would normally meet at golf and country clubs to discuss national matters.

They advised the president to lead from the front in stemming the open disapproval of his leadership before it got out of hand.

The State Research Bureau was established for this purpose. The Special Branch, an offshoot of the Criminal Investigation Department, was tasked with sending field agents to put their ear on the ground, to collect data and to read the general mood of the country.

In addition, the district administrators were given youth wingers to help them in disseminating government propaganda.

Bwana Kamangu, who had served previously in the colonial government, had now been made the district commissioner by the new regime. He was given his quota of youth wingers payrolled by the government to assist him in carrying out the important task of nation building.

The only thing that seemed to distract Juma from his gripe with the government was his friendship with Mumbi, which had grown by leaps and bounds since she left school two years ago.

Waciuri had played a big role in their courtship because he had become the errand boy when Mumbi needed to send letters to Juma. Usually, it was difficult for them to meet as often as they wished because of her father's restrictions.

Mumbi's father's intention was to send his daughter to the capital city to further her education and he could not allow that dream to be shattered by her getting impregnated by the young men in the village. He therefore instructed his wife to keep a close eye on their daughter.

One evening, when Waciuri was returning from the market, he passed by Mumbi's home to collect the bag of maize flour that she had told him to take to his grandmother.

What made him remember to collect the maize flour though was because Juma had a message for Mumbi that he wanted him to give her. He told him to inform her that they should meet the following market day.

"Good evening Mumbi, I came from the market on my way home when I remembered you wanted me to collect the bag of maize flour," Waciuri said.

"Principal Juma also sent me to tell you to meet him at the ridge near the waterfall the next market day," he added as an afterthought.

"Thank you. Let me get you the bag of maize, I'm not going to invite you for tea as it is getting late and I don't want you to travel in the dark," she replied.

"I shall take the tea some other day," Waciuri replied back.

When he was given the bag, he slung it on his back and waved Mumbi goodbye. "Greet *cucu* for me when you get home," Mumbi said as she waved back.

When he finally got home, it was already dark and the chickens had gone home to roost on the mango tree in the compound.

His grandmother was busy preparing the evening meal by stirring the steaming stew with a wooden laddle and her brow was covered with sweat.

His grandfather was keeping her company by trying to strike a conversation but it was mostly a monologue. He could as well have been talking to himself.

"Where did you get the money to buy the bag of maize flour?" Waciuri's grandmother asked when he got to the kitchen.

"Good evening," Waciuri greeted both his grandparents as he put down the bag and whatever else he carried with him.

"Even those guinea fowls that you take to the market cannot earn you enough to buy that much quantity of maize flour," his grandfather chipped in.

"I was given this by Bwana Kamangu's daughter Mumbi to give to *cucu*," he replied as he grabbed the other remaining stool to sit on and join them for dinner.

"May God do to her as she has done to us, that girl will turn out to become a great woman for her good heart," Waciuri's grandmother said as she scooped some stew with the ladle to taste if the food was ready.

"One would not imagine that she is Kamangu's daughter. They are poles apart," Waciuri's grandfather observed.

When dinner was ready and served, Waciuri watched the funny shadows of their figures on the kitchen's wall.

From the different positions that each one of them sat, they cast different shadows. *Guka*'s (grandfather) shadow had his body stretched long with a big shapeless head.

Cucu's shadow had a small pressed body like that of a warthog's with an even smaller head.

His looked monstrous like the one eyed ogres that his grandmother usually mentioned in her fables.

***

Mr. Njagah, the area MP for Mutituini who had won with a landslide running on a DDP ticket, was rarely seen in his constituency.

Indeed, any contender who ran on a DDP ticket was assured of being voted in because of the euphoria the people had of having to elect their own people to govern them instead of the oppressive colonial government.

The other reason that ensured that those who run on a DDP ticket won is the campaign slogan that they employed, mostly that it was the leader of the party and the party's war veterans who fought for their independence.

So people voted three-piece, that is to say they voted in the president, the area MP and the district administrator from the same party.

That is perhaps what saw Bwana Kamangu sail in, despite his personality.

After Njagah was elected in, he started acquiring new friends in the city, influential politicians and businessmen. He now had no time for simple villagers.

He therefore spent more time in the city than in his constituency. When on rare occasions his needy constituents managed to get a hold of him to seek his assistance, he would tell them that the reason he spent more time in the city was because he was busy representing them in parliament. However, he had never presented a single bill for debate in parliament.

Today he was having a lunch meeting with his counterpart Bwana Kamangu at his residence.

"I hear that people here are only talking politics instead of working. We should find a way of making them cut down on the anti- government rhetoric," Mr. Njagah told Bwana Kamangu as he was carving out a generous juicy piece from a roasted goats' leg.

"I have instructed my boys," as he was fond of calling his youth wingers, "to attend all *barazas* and call off all meetings that are political in nature," Bwana Kamangu replied as he picked his teeth to remove some pieces of goat meat lodged between them. This was making him uncomfortable after eating such a sumptuous meal.

"You know when all party MPs, were summoned to the last party meeting, the secretariat mentioned that they would send over agents of the state to monitor the situation on the ground if we are not able to contain the situation in our respective areas," added Mr. Njagah.

"So I heard, my boys will see to it that people here tone down on their views. When will they work if all they do is talk politics?" Bwana Kamangu pointed out.

"I have instructed them to summon those people who do not heed that directive to my office. They should leave politics to us, that's the reason for which we are paid, to represent them," he added.

Since the youth wingers became part of the local administration in the various localities, they had become a loathed lot by the villagers because of their interference in their personal affairs.

Land disputes or marital disagreements that would normally be solved by village elders or the respective religious leaders in an amicable way were now taken to the youth wingers for arbitration by people who knew they would not get a favourable decision.

For example, those people who had a greedy eye on their neighbour's land would take their complaints to the youth wingers regarding the placement of land beacons that divided their farms.

They would not even consult the services of land surveyors who were trained in such issues.

The reason that they would prefer the youth wingers is that they made skewed judgements in their favour when they greased their palms with bribes.

The youth wingers would justify such corruption by saying among themselves that it all started from the top and that it was their opportunity to 'eat' before the tap ran dry.

They were also despised because, lately, they were interfering with the democratic right of people to assemble and discuss how political events were shaping up in their nation.

***

Mumbi was taking particularly long to dress up on this particular market day. She had found an excuse to give to her mother to allow her to go to the market.

Her father had gone to the city to mind some family business and her mother would sometimes grant her such requests because she also found her husband's restrictions on her daughter's movements stifling.

It was the market day that she had a date with Principal Juma, and she wanted to make a good impression on him.

Today, she applied a generous amount of coconut oil on her cropped hair and sweet scented oil on her body.

She found him near the waterfall as he had instructed and she could see his face brighten up when she showed up. He wasn't sure if Waciuri had remembered to pass the message to her but here she was.

When she saw him, she too smiled sheepishly and her dimples came out as usual.

When they got close, he did not greet her in their usual manner but rather stooped to hug her and plant a kiss on her lips.

She was pleasantly surprised and let the moment linger for a few seconds before she snapped back to the world. He then reluctantly released her.

"I've missed you. We don't meet as often as possible," Juma said with a smile on his face.

"I know. I don't get an opportunity to see you. You know how dad is," she replied.

"I know your father wants to send you to the city to further your education. I don't have a problem with that, but I think he should not choose who you decide to see or not, that decision lies with you, you are an adult," Juma added.

"The distance will not erase the memories, and I'm willing to wait on you and get married to you. No one can make me feel the same way I feel towards you," she replied.

That sunny afternoon, they sat down on the verdant grass and talked about their future together. Juma was doing most of the talking and Mumbi listened while shyly twirling a blade of grass where she sat.

Against the soothing soundtrack of the waterfall and the chirping of different bird species, it was the perfect backdrop and they both wished the moment would last forever.

That night when she went to bed, she put her fingers to her lips as she thought about the kiss. It was her very first and she could swear that she could smell his manly ardour lingering on her lips.

Juma was whistling cheerfully as one who had won a lottery while doing his dishes after having his dinner.

He looked forward to the day when Mumbi would be the one doing the dishes he was now washing.

Chapter Seven

It was now four years since president Sonkoh came to power and corruption had now become endemic in government and was now devolving down to the private sector.

The back bench in parliament, which was the unofficial opposition, was stifled by the majority in the house. When they tried to point out corrupt deals in government ministries like phantom deals that were entered into with international companies- which were costing the government tax payers monies-, they were quickly shot down by the impunity of the majority.

Well connected people would win tenders to provide services or build infrastructures like roads and hospitals and there would be nothing much to show after the stipulated time of completion.

Detention without trial, a practise that was perpetrated by the colonial government, was now creeping in. People would be arrested and taken to the capital city for questioning the current leadership.

When people met in social places, they talked in hushed tones and would avoid discussing the president's style of leadership with strangers lest they be state agents.

Things were moving from bad to worse. At least even during the colonial government, people would discuss politics openly without expecting government retribution.

But now, it was difficult to discuss politics freely; one had to look over his shoulder to see who was around. People had to confirm the safety of their surroundings.

Elected leaders would engage in sycophancy and sing praises to their dear president in order to gain favours. And even choir masters would compose patriotic songs that praised the good leadership of their president.

There was now clamour for elections by the populace that was due next year as stipulated in the constitution. The constitution stipulated that elections be held every five years.

The president was going for one of those tours that he normally did once in a while to meet the people and see government projects around the country.

Among the places in his diary that he was to visit was the largest mental hospital in the country.

It was supposed to be a surprise visit to see if government institutions were efficient in the provision of services to the people. But as usual, the state comptroller had tipped those places that the head of state would pay a visit so that they should get their house in order and avoid embarrassing the president.

The route that the president was taking was lined up with school children who sang praises when he passed.

When he got near the state run hospital, he saw a multitude of people waving at him and ordered his motorcade to stop so that he could greet his people.

He got out and waved his *rungu* (club), which he always carried with him when meeting his subjects. It signified leadership in the African culture.

"I hear that there is clamour for multiparty elections. The wind always carries words back to me," he told the crowd.

He told them that with the different tribes in the country, multiparty politics would only divide them because they would be tribal outfits.

He then asked the crowd "are you ready for multiparty politics?"

They roared back "no!" They wanted to tell him what he wanted to hear hoping that they would get handouts that he would sometimes dish out when doing the meet-the- people tour.

"Do you want another president?" he asked again.

"Sonkoh for life!" they roared back.

He then told them better the devil you know than the angel that you don't.

His retinue of ministers clapped enthusiastically for his wisdom, or so they thought.

When the president finally got to the mental hospital, he was taken on a guided tour by the hospital administrators to see that the facility was spotlessly cleaned.

He could see the mental patients with their clean green khaki uniforms lazing around in the wards.

He then came up to one particular patient who seemed oblivious of his visit.

"Do you know who I am?" the president asked the patient.

The patient asked him who he was and he replied "Sonkoh, the president of Donyokeri."

"You are in the right place. I also used to say that I was Sonkoh before I was brought here," the patient said.

The entourage stifled their laughter, and when the president read the mood he replied "like we say in our culture, every market place has its own madman."

They all burst out in laughter that they had suppressed earlier.

***

Waciuri had now cleared primary school and was looking forward to entering secondary school.

It was during the school holidays that he went through circumcision rites that now saw him graduate into a young man.

He would now cease to go for deer hunting and trapping guinea fowls and would engage in other manly activities, which would involve, among other things, trying to court girls of his own age group.

They would waylay the girls as they were going to the river to fetch water and try to woo them with long tales, and the girls would giggle among themselves because the lads seemed to be making fools of themselves.

Chapter Eight

Karen Country Club was the most expensive and exclusive club in the country. It was patronized by the who-is-who in the country.

Those with membership in the country club included some of the ministers in the government, settlers who had opted to stay because of their vast investments in the country and expatriates.

This is where the president and members of his "kitchen cabinet" had gone to meet this particular Sunday. Some of the members of the kitchen cabinet included the Minister of Defence and Home Affairs, and the Attorney General, among others.

They normally met once in a while to discuss matters of the state and business in general over some drinks. The drink of choice for most of them was *Tusker* beer, but Ngei, the Minister for Defence and Home Affairs, liked his Highland Park scotch whisky.

It was one year to elections since the country gained independence four years ago and the clamour for elections was gaining momentum from the people.

From the intelligence that he got, people were still calling for elections despite his appeals that having multiple political parties would divide the country.

Even though the country was governed as a one party state with no effective opposition, the law still allowed for multiparty politics. And that was the topic of discussion on this particular day.

"This call for others to run against me is becoming an irritant. What are the chances of us losing an election?" the president asked no one in particular.

"No one can beat you in an election! We have the

state machinery to run an effective campaign!" Ngei, the Minister for Defence replied in a loud and excitable voice.

Clearly the scotch whisky had taken its toll on Ngei, who usually talked this way when he had taken one too many.

"Still, we cannot take our chances," the amiable AG Mr. Johnson, who had been retained from the previous colonial government, chipped in.

"What if donor countries decide to finance the opposition," he added.

"Those racists would not dare! We shall not allow ourselves to be colonized through the back door! That is neocolonialism!" Ngei shot back deliriously.

"The easier option would be to repeal a section of the constitution which would make the country effectively a one party state," the AG proffered.

The president agreed that this was the best option instead of engaging in a demanding election.

And so, with the stroke of a pen, Donyokeri, which was a *de facto* one party state, was turned into a *de jure* one party state.

***

When the back bench in parliament, the unofficial opposition, learned about this coup, there was a furore, with their members threatening that they would not support government bills and would call their constituents to protest or stop paying taxes altogether.

The media was not left behind, and this turn of events provided fodder for their editorial opinions.

Finally, word went round the country of what had happened and the reaction was predictable. After peasants were informed by the likes of Juma in the *barazas* of what had taken place, people began protesting, and carrying twigs in the town's streets and village paths, and singing, "*Haki yetu! Haki yetu!* "(Our rights! Our rights!)

The reaction from the government was swift. Police were unleashed on them and they shot tear gas canisters, chased and clobbered the protestors who were scampering helter-skelter in all directions. Even old mothers were not spared.

Juma was one of those arrested for addressing people under the great *mugumo* (fig) tree where villagers usually converged to attend a *baraza*.

He was taken to the local police post and held there as he waited to be taken to court the following day.

"You trouble maker! We know you! Just because you have read papers you think you can overthrow the government by holding *barazas* under a tree?" Onyango, the police chief of the local post mocked Juma.

"My brother, take it easy and concentrate on your teaching job if you don't want trouble from the government," Onyango added. They came from the same area in Siala and he thought a little cautionary advice was fitting.

The following day, Juma was taken to court, charged with convening an illegal assembly and slapped with a heavy fine of ten thousand shillings or six months in jail in default.

Luckily for him, a *harambee* (fundraising) was quickly held to raise the money for the fine by the villagers and he was set free much to the chagrin of the local administration.

From then on, Juma was a marked man. Even though the Special Branch tried their best to remain discrete, he could tell it was them when he went for a drink at *Kahuti* Bar and Rest because of the ill-fitting suits which made them standout from other patrons.

They also tended to keep to themselves even when having drinks.

He now had to be careful, and would in future meet like-minded friends in his school house in the guise of discussing the development of education in Mutituini.

Just like the arrests that took place in the rest of the country to deal with the protestors, Mumbi was to learn later about the arrest of Juma when she heard her father tell her mother that they would not entertain inciters in his village.

She would have to talk to Juma and implore him to tone down his politicking even though she was aware it wasn't easy to convince him, especially when he felt strongly about an issue.

That resoluteness was one of the qualities she liked about him because it brought out the determined character in him but she feared that it would one day cause him trouble.

***

After the long December holidays, Waciuri entered Jamhuri Secondary School as a first former.

The transition from primary to secondary school was a milestone for him. He had now graduated from using slates to writing in exercise books, there were two additional subjects, geography and science and he had to contend with being bullied as a rite of passage for any first former.

Principal Juma, having been acquainted to Waciuri - for the errand runs that he carried out for him - had made his transition to secondary school much easier by picking a senior student to protect him from bullying. Even though it would happen sometimes, he did not make a fuss about it and took it in stride.

This endeared him to the other students because it showed that he was not seeking special favours and was aware of the tradition.

Principal Juma had started hosting some of his like-minded colleagues and drinking mates at his house in the evening after school every Friday. They would take dinner and have drinks as they discussed the political events in the country.

It was the fifth year since the country gained independence, and elections should have been held later that year had it not been for the repeal of a statute in the constitution that had effectively turned the country into a single-party state.

"So dear comrades, our leaders have stolen our dream and run with it," Juma addressed his friends who were lounging on the seats in the living room of his house.

"And the sad thing is that those who fought the settlers for their injustices are doing the same things," Bildad, the youthful entrepreneur who had started his business by opening a retail shop, which later grew to a wholesale shop, pointed out. His glass clinked when it made contact with the bottle of whitecap beer as he was replenishing his empty glass.

Muthoni, a colleague of Juma in the school, sat quietly, swirling her glass of dark oily Guinness beer as she thought pensively.

Muthoni had lost both of her parents during the emergency period. They were killed by home-guards after being accused of being collaborators with the freedom fighters.

The home-guards had been their neighbours and had falsely accused her parents so that they could inherit their piece of land. She loathed them as equally as she loathed the colonial government.

She was raised by a missionary school run by the Anglican Church after she became orphaned. Her other siblings were inherited by her relatives and she was the only one who ended up getting an education and train as a teacher.

She had not imagined that those who took over after the British left would have included home-guards, who had oppressed them in their government. Perhaps it was the reason that the Uhuru dream had stalled.

The others in the room, who were at different stages of inebriation, sat chatting among themselves.

"Dear friends, I want to inform you that I have made contact with the other progressive groups around the country and we have agreed to form an alliance so as to present our issues to the government with one voice," Juma told them after hitting his glass with a spoon to get their attention.

"We have agreed to name the alliance, People of Donyokeri Alliance-PDA," he added.

And the discussion progressed late into the night as their voices and music - which was playing on the gramophone - got louder as alcohol took its toll on them.

Chapter Nine

Donor countries, namely the US and the European Union, had been following events in the country through regular cable updates from their respective embassies.

They closely followed the autocratic misrule of president Sonkoh and when he would travel to those countries to discuss bilateral agreements, the host presidents of those countries would urge him to open up democratic space and especially fight the endemic corruption in his country.

He would of course tell them how his government was working hard to address these issues. But after the country changed to a one party state by law, donor countries began freezing aid to it in order to force the government to rethink the decision.

MacClare, the Minister for Trade who had been nominated by the president, was clandestinely feeding government information to his foreign masters in the West.

MacClare, a bulky six foot man, was a talkative and engaging fellow with a rather acerbic tongue.

He was a socialite and would always be found in dinner parties mingling with the guests when foreign countries held their Independence Day celebrations in their respective embassy grounds.

He was also a member of the cabinet in Sonkoh's government and made a point of attending every time they met. However, the inner circle that surrounded the president did not embrace him because they felt they could not trust him.

However, he had a good working relationship with Ngei, the Minister for Defence and Home Affairs, and they got along quite well. Perhaps it was because they both shared their love for whiskey.

This would prove very important because it was on such occasions when they were having drinks that he would glean information that would prove useful to his foreign masters. They called it "high value intel."

For example, the foreign community was watching with keen interest the group of young educated men and women who had formed an alliance to advocate for change in the country and would be willing to help if the need arose.

***

At sunrise, Mumbi was in the kitchen busy going through her usual morning ritual of preparing breakfast for her family.

She had poured some milk, which she got from one of their dairy cows christened Daisy, on the kettle atop the cooker and she added an equal amount of water sprinkled with a generous spoonful amount of tea leaves. Two slices of bread were toasting in the grill of the cooker. Just like her father liked his bread.

Daisy, a white and brown Guernsey cow, was the one that was picked out among the rest of the herd to provide milk for Bwana Kamangu's household. The rest of the milk from the large number of dairy cattle was sold to a dairy company.

Since clearing school, she would keep herself busy in their house doing chores to kill boredom. And preparing breakfast was one of the chores.

As she struck a match to light the burner that held the kettle of tea, her thoughts wandered to Juma.

She had to see him to discuss the issue of his safety, which had been bothering her lately. She would have to find an excuse to give so as to leave the house.

She snapped back from her thoughts when the

boiling tea, which was now rising, hit the lid of the kettle with a hissing sound as some of it spilled onto the burner. She switched off the cooker instantly, just when her mother was entering the kitchen.

"You look distracted nowadays, what is the matter?" her mother enquired when she smelt the smell of burning milk that had spilled on the burner.

"It's nothing mom," Mumbi replied as she was setting the kettle and cups on a tray.

"I hope there is nothing wrong, or are you pregnant?" her mother pressed on with a tinge of worry in her voice.

"No mum, I was just a little bit distracted, that's all," she answered back with a smile to reassure her mother.

"This absent-mindedness will one day make you forget your own child in the market place when you become a mother," said her mother as she left the kitchen after picking what she came for.

***

That year was unusually dry as the long rains of the months of April to July had failed to come as expected, and the villagers were getting anxious about their crop in the field.

If things continued like this, they would be forced to eat yellow maize again like they had reluctantly done some years back when the colonial government had imported it after the country had faced a particularly severe drought.

Those who were around during that drought particularly remember it because it was so severe. Children were so malnourished that their hair turned a silver hue. They developed scurvy and were forced to scavenge for wild fruits. It was called the famine of the cassava.

Before cock crow, when the orange cold light of early morning glinted the skies, Waciuri would be already up at dawn heading to the river to fetch water for his grandmother and would be back in time to milk the only cow before leaving for school.

The morning harmattan wind was not particularly good for his frail grandmother because of her age and he would therefore not let her wake up early to milk the cow or walk to the riverbank to fetch water.

In those days, the rivers were unpolluted. He would visit a stream to fetch water for his grandmother and drink water straight from the stream with his open palms.

He would try in vain to pick the strands of frogs' eggs which looked like beads. But every time he put his little fingers under them, they would break.

On subsequent visits to the river, he saw hundreds of tadpoles - black, energetic and wriggling through the clear water.

He would also help in tilling the farm, sowing and harvesting the crops that they would have planted that season, and repairing the granary to ensure that the harvested cereals did not get depleted by mice or weevils.

He was therefore very useful in the home, and his grandmother always prayed to her ancestors to bless her only grandson for his industriousness.

Waciuri's hard work was not only limited at home but he was equally good in academics at Jamhuri Secondary School. He was also a good athlete and participated in both sprinting and handball.

Some weekends, principal Juma would ask him to accompany him to the market to purchase rations and drinks for his friends who congregated at his house to chat on current affairs. He would linger around and insist on helping.

His reason for wanting to hang around was that he enjoyed listening to their debates. This had a profound impact on him as he came to understand how the politics of a few could affect the lives of millions of people either positively or otherwise.

"The assurance by the government that it has enough maize reserve is hogwash. Do you know that there is a maize shortage in the country? I'm selling the last bags in my shop," Waciuri heard Bildad bellow as he was Helping Teacher Muthoni set the table.

"The politicians are busy enriching themselves while impoverishing the masses," Juma interjected.

"Maybe what this country needs is a revolution," Muthoni chipped in as she always did when Juma raised a point. Waciuri had also noticed that Teacher Muthoni always stared admiringly when Juma raised a point.

"A revolution is not an apple that falls when it is ripe, you have to make it fall" the revolutionary Wafula, who had a crush on the bootilicious dark-complexioned Muthoni, quoted Che Guevara, a Marxist revolutionary he had read about, to make an impression.

Juma concurred with him and observed that those who make a peaceful revolution impossible will one day make a violent revolution inevitable.

***

It was the end of the second term and schools had closed for the holidays when the government began stamping on dissidents.

They started with Rukuna, the capital city, before swiftly moving to the provinces. Members of the People of Donyokeri Alliance were rounded up and taken to detention centres around the country.

They were held incommunicado as their charges were prepared for involving themselves in subversive activities against an elected government. They were later taken to court in the evening and with only the prosecutor and the judge present, the charges were read to them.

Of course, none pleaded guilty and the overzealous prosecutor asked the court for more time to carry out more investigations

They were blindfolded by the Special Branch officers as they sat sandwiched by two officers at the back seat of the infamous Peugeot 504's and taken around the city centre and the outskirts for hours to disorient them. Sometimes, they were bundled in the boot of the car and told to *"Ka square!"*(To take the foetal position in order to fit in the boot).

Finally, they were taken to the State Research Bureau for a little "coaxing" to jog their memories.

The State Research Bureau was built in a secluded wooded neighbourhood in one of the affluent areas in the city, and residents who did their early morning runs could swear that they always heard people wailing in the rather serene compound.

Curiosity got the better of some of them who would go to enquire what was happening. They would be met at the sturdy wrought iron gate by mean looking men in dark suits who would tell them to mind their own business or go and make a formal complaint to the police if they so wished.

What baffled people was the number of vehicles getting in or leaving at odd hours even though they never saw the occupants because the vehicles had tinted windows.

***

Mumbi did not sleep well that night. She was tossing and turning in her bed most of the night and she decided to go prepare a cup of hot chocolate. Maybe that would help her get some sleep.

She had a trepidation that something was not quite right but she could not figure what it was. Anyway, she grabbed her night gown and made her way to the kitchen.

As she was going to the kitchen, she heard muffled voices coming from the study room and she realised it was her father's.

Her father did not normally work this late into the night and she got curious. She tiptoed to the study and for sure it was her father on the phone.

And then she heard it. "Sure, that fool has been hosting people in his house clandestinely," her father spoke on the mouth-piece of the phone.

"Yes, yes we have been monitoring him and I think tomorrow in the office would be fine, we don't want to cause a scene, the students might riot or something," he added before slamming the receiver back to its cradle and going back to what he was doing before the interruption.

She held her open mouth in fear and tiptoed back to her bedroom, almost tripping over a coffee table in the foyer.

"So that was the reason she felt uneasy," she thought. She would go by the break of dawn to Juma's place to warn him. It did not matter what her father would say later if he found out she had left the house without seeking his permission.

That night, she did not sleep until guinea fowls and turkeys in their homestead began to chuckle early in the morning. If anything happened to Juma, she would always blame herself.

***

Very early the next morning, Mumbi made her way to Juma's house and was surprised when no one answered her knock, even after rapping the door with anxious urgency for a while.

She sat on the verandah dejectedly and with fear written all over her face. She had herself to blame. If only she had told their night watchman to accompany her to Juma's house the previous night, they would not have arrested him.

As she was returning back home, she met Gumba, their watchman. "Where have you been? Your father is raving mad asking if anyone has seen you," he asked her with an urgent tone to his voice.

"I left just when the night watchman left," she sullenly answered.

"Madam, hei! You will cost us our jobs, boss has been raving and ranting," Gumba pleaded.

"Don't worry, I will take the blame, it was not your fault anyway," Mumbi reassured him as they went back home.

"Young woman! Where have you been?" her father snarled when they finally got home.

"Have you started sneaking out and sleeping around? Didn't I warn you about the village brats?" her father continued.

Mumbi tried to explain. "Dad it wasn't like that, I ..."

"Are you trying to embarrass me after all I've done for you? I'll take you to the city the soonest possible," her father cut her short.

"I do not want to hear anything from you, get out of my sight!" he yelled.

Chapter Ten

The next morning the president chaired a security meeting with the Minister for Defence and Home Affairs, the Commissioner of Police and other high profile security chiefs in the respective departments.

They briefed him on the operations of the previous few days and told him it was just a matter of time before they rounded up all the dissidents.

"The only problem is the backlash from the international community," Ngei, the Minister of Defence, pointed out.

"That will be taken care of," the president said. "We don't need their money anyway. We can always look East for new bilateral partners."

"They give loans without strings attached. They call it non-interference with the internal affairs of sovereign nations," the president added with raucous laughter.

… two days earlier, MacClare, the Minister for Trade, had gotten the intel of the operation. It was a top secret government affair only known to a few people in the cabinet and security apparatus. He had passed the information to a trusted person who was charged with passing sensitive information to the scouts who worked hand-in-hand with reform groups like the PDA.

The message was passed by phone to the respective cell leaders through coded language, and that was how Juma, managed to get it the same day before the operation in his village.

He received a call from his office telephone just when he was about to leave for the day and was told that- 'chickens will be coming home to roost.' He instantly understood the hidden message.

He immediately got in touch with his friends and they

hid in a safe house awaiting further instructions.

After the president left the meeting, the others did not leave immediately because they wanted to discuss further.

The head of the Special Branch told them that he felt that there was a mole among them as they had only managed to take in half of all the dissidents. After all, no one else apart from those in the room knew about the operation code-named Cobra. He would soon carry out his own investigations, he thought to himself.

***

Juma and his team were holed up in a friend's house on the fringes of Mutituini near the snow capped Ol Donyo Keri Mountain.

Before he came to the safe house, he passed by Waciuri's home and informed him that he would like him to take a short trip to the coastal town, Mula, and be back in time before the schools opened.

He was to collect some money the following day for his train fare at Bildad's general shop, but first he had to travel to Bahati Estate in the city, – Rukuna, and ask for Njoroge the charcoal dealer, by hiking a lift on Bildad's lorry.

Juma decided to send Waciuri because he was young and could therefore raise less suspicion. He also felt that he could count on him because he had dealt with him before on errands and found him reliable.

He also told him not to tell anyone of his whereabouts, not even Mumbi, at least for the time being.

And so that night, Waciuri sat cross-legged on his stool in the kitchen opposite his grandmother.

Between them, - sat an earthen pot with boiling water on a three-stoned *jiko* (stove).

She was peeling potatoes and arrow-roots and

dropping them in the pot. Somewhere outside, crickets were chirping.

"*Cucu,* why don't people in the government act to arrest the famine situation in the country?" he engaged his grandmother in small talk before giving her the news of his short trip.

He was roasting some cob maize by placing them on one of the stones near some burning firewood.

"When the leader sheep limps, the herd does not reach the pasture," she replied to the question as she always did with parables.

His grandfather had retired earlier to bed and informed his grandmother that he would take his dinner the following day.

"*Cucu*, I wanted to inform you that I will be travelling on a short trip to the city and be back before the schools open," he finally said after clearing his throat for the fifth time.

"Are you travelling with some friends...and have you informed your grandfather?"

"Well, I'm...yes, and that's why I told you. I want you to talk to grandfather about it."

The following morning, with a bag strapped on one of his shoulders, he hugged both his grandparents as he bade them farewell.

"It is only the person who does not travel that says that his mother is the best cook," his grandfather said philosophically as Waciuri hugged him.

He stepped over the crooked wooden gate of their hedge fence, looked over his shoulder one last time and watched their house disappear as he walked away towards the market.

PART TWO

Early Seventies

Chapter Eleven

Walking towards Mutituini on the village path, Waciuri could not help but admire the rustic idyllic environment that was his home town.

Both sides of the red dusty road were surrounded by rusty undulating hills. Had it rained as expected, the hills would be clothed with a blanket of lush green plantations dotted with hamlets.

The circular thatched huts were now more visible because of the almost bare landscape.

Vehicles would occasionally pass by, ferrying passengers on their way to the city, leaving a cloud of lazy rising red dust behind. Whenever Waciuri saw a vehicle approaching, he would move to the furthest side of the road after jumping the ditches created on each side. The ditches picked up the torrents of rain water when it rained, which helped to keep the earthen road less muddy.

He jumped the ditches on to the furthest side to avoid the dust because he didn't want his clothes getting dusty before he even got to the city.

He finally got to the market and found his way to Bildad's shop where he met his wife serving customers at the counter.

"Yes Waciuri, we have been expecting you," she said as she was handing change to one of the customers.

"Just sit on the bench. I'll get you a *fanta* (soda) and a loaf of bread as you wait for the loaders to finish loading," she added.

When they had finished loading, Bildad's wife gave Waciuri fare money for his trip to Mula. He was to pick the train in Rukuna.

"Take care and remember to go to Bahati Estate and ask for Njoroge, the charcoal dealer," she said as she was bidding him farewell.

"Yes mum, I'll remember," he replied as he waved back.

The driver was already on the seat of the turquoise coloured Bedford lorry. The engine was running.

The loader helped Waciuri climb into the lorry's cabin as he followed suite and sat sandwiched between them on their way to Rukuna.

***

The ambassadors representing the international community- or what they used to call themselves partners of Donyokeri- held a joint press conference condemning the harsh crack down of citizens expressing their opinions.

They called for the government to respect freedom of speech and assembly, and to concentrate more on averting the looming disaster in the making: famine

Juma and his friends spent most of the day holed up in the living room of their friend's house as they followed the political development in their country and the political fallout from the international community.

They did this through the radio by changing channels from local ones to the BBC. Apparently, their host did not have a battery powered TV, unlike some of the villagers.

Bildad was one of the few lucky ones who owned one, but could not risk going to his house now that they were fugitives running away from the government's security machinery.

Also, going to the shop would put the lives of his wife and workers at risk and so Bildad had to contend with their host's spartan living standards.

"The international community should do more

instead of making simple statements, like cutting diplomatic ties," Juma observed as he strained his ear on the Sanyo radio.

"Yes, that's the kind of language that they understand," Muthoni seconded.

When Juma was not following the unfolding situation, he was thinking of Mumbi and missing her terribly.

Wafula was helping the host prepare dinner by plucking the feathers of the chicken he had just slaughtered and dipping it in hot water to make the plucking easier.

Chapter Twelve

It was a gloomy morning and the clouds were dark and heavy. It seemed that the heavens would open up eventually.

Mumbi was despondent. Her father had made arrangements for her to move to the city centre as he had threatened.

He had even secured a secretarial college for her and paid the requisite fees. He clearly wanted her out of the village.

The only consolation, if any, was that she could probably try to locate where the police had taken Juma and find out how he was doing, that is, if they would allow her in the first place.

Meanwhile, Juma had been replaced in the school by the mathematics teacher who was now the acting principal.

The Ministry of Education had sent Juma a suspension letter for dereliction of duty, pending dismissal.

The students learnt of the unfortunate turn of events and were distraught because Principal Juma was a popular and likeable teacher and they would really miss his geography classes.

***

When they arrived in Rukuna, it was already dark and they had to find accommodation for the night.

Waciuri was fascinated by night time in the city centre. The neon lights made the city look like a moonlit night back in the village but without stars in the skies, only this time; the people did not seem to retire to their homes to sleep.

People seemed to be in a hurry even at this time of the day, as if the following day would not come for them to finish whatever errands they had.

And when they got to Tea Room Guest House, where they were to spend the night, he saw skimpily dressed women waving and winking at them even though they were strangers. He waved back thinking people in the city were really friendly.

The following morning, as he parted ways with the lorry crew, they told him to ask the bus conductor for directions and no one else. They told him people from the city were not to be trusted and if they found out he was new in the city, they would con him out of his money in the pretence of helping him.

People in the city seemed to be in even more of a hurry during the day as if each of them was late for an appointment, Waciuri thought.

Waciuri waded through the streets heading to the bus station to look for a bus conductor to ask for directions to Bahati estate. He found one on a bus that was waiting to fill up.

He had a metallic ticket machine slung on one of his tired shoulders and looked fatigued.

"Excuse me, where is the bus that plies Bahati estate?" Waciuri enquired.

The conductor wearily gave him the number of the bus that plied the route to Bahati.

After the conductor called for those alighting at Bahati, he alighted from the Leyland bus and went ahead to ask around for directions to Njoroge's yard - the one who sold charcoal.

He finally arrived at the charcoal yard but did not find Njoroge as he had expected. However, he found his employee who told him that his boss had gone to make a delivery and would come back soon.

He sat on a hard pavement nearby waiting for Njoroge to come back so he could give him the message that he was to take with him to Mula.

Chapter Thirteen

Otieno, one of the leaders of People of Donyokeri Alliance (PDA) in the city, and other members who had been arrested and blindfolded were headed to the State Research Bureau.

On arrival, they were taken to the basement's pitch-dark dungeons and stripped naked. They were held in waterlogged cells for days and were sprayed with cold water from a powerful hosepipe.

Sometimes a powerful light would be flashed on their faces, blinding them temporarily.

Otieno had spent ten days standing in the waterlogged cells, surviving only on a loaf of bread that was brought once in the morning.

Sometimes, he would drop because of exhaustion and sleep and wake up abruptly once he fell into the cold water.

"I have spent days standing in water, that is when you know how long a night is," Otieno thought to himself.

He was woken from his thoughts when a woman in high heels entered and ordered him to follow her.

He shielded his eyes from the glare of the light in the corridor with his hands, having spent days in the darkness, opening his eyes slowly as he tried to adjust to the light.

"My friend, just confess and implicate the others and things will be easier for you," the officer cajoled as she fondled him whilst they were walking along the corridor.

He was ushered into a big empty room with only a chair in the middle and six chairs and a desk in front.

He was ordered to sit on the middle chair. In front sat six men.

The look on their faces left no doubt in his mind that at some stage, the encounter would develop into a violent and vicious confrontation.

"Why do you want to overthrow the government," one burly officer, who he was to later learn was called Opiyo and was their leader, asked.

Otieno protested that he had not eaten for days and was given a loaf of bread and cigarettes.

"If you cooperate, you will go back to the warmth of your family, who I'm sure are very anxious of your whereabouts by now," Opiyo continued.

"I don't see how our meeting to discuss political events in our country is trying to overthrow the government," replied Otieno.

"So you think you are right and the rest of Donyokerians are wrong," Opiyo continued his interrogation.

"The constitution allows for freedom of assem..." his reply was interrupted when Opiyo picked up one of the wooden chairs and hit him and the others descended on him with whips and blows.

It was the beginning of an endless journey of torture.

After collapsing, he was dragged and thrown back into the dungeons. The second day he would undergo the same treatment, only that the tactics would change.

One day, they removed pistols and threatened to shoot him, and he had no doubt in his mind that they would carry out their threat as others had been shot during interrogation.

But he refused to confess that he was engaging in subversive activities. He also refused to implicate others. He was taken back to the dungeons and he could hear screams in neighbouring cells. He eventually lost count of days and time.

But of course, there are those who succumbed to the physical and mental torture, the threats, and humiliations, and had confessed.

They would be taken to court, where their tormentors stood as witnesses, and be sentenced to various prison terms.

Otieno's father, who had a long standing condition of heart disease, had collapsed and died of a stroke when he learnt that his eldest son - who they relied on - had been taken in by state security agents.

***

Mumbi was finally taken to the city centre to start her secretarial course and was to put up with some relatives in the city.

Her relatives received her warmly and treated her as one of their own as was common in the African society. No child was exclusively owned by their own parents; instead, the whole community took the responsibility of rearing and disciplining other children as they would their own.

That night when she went to bed, she thought about Juma and could not reconcile herself to the fact that here she was sleeping comfortably while Juma was sleeping on some hard cold cell floor.

She was kept awake by the curious conviction that something significant was about to happen. Something was sliding, or spinning towards her through the darkness.

She wept her heart out and thought her father cruel and inconsiderate. Finally, however, she fell into a deep sleep.

Chapter Fourteen

Waciuri finally met Njoroge and was given the message that he was to take to Mula. He was to ask specifically for James who worked at the port as a clerk, to deliver the message.

He took a bus back to the city centre and weaved his way to the train station, where he bought a ticket for Mula at one of the several counters after standing for a while in a long winding queue.

Passengers were jostling to get into the train as the station officers tried to control them; others tried to get wailing children through the train windows after having left them behind in the confusion.

Finally amid the din, Waciuri managed to get a seat next to a window as he had hoped and waited patiently, for what seemed like eternity, before the train slowly lurched out of the station after its horn made a long choo choo sound to warn people to move away from it.

They travelled and began to lose sight of the city as they started encountering scrub land and trees flew by. The wind whistled by as they moved into the wilderness.

Waciuri was glad he had secured a seat next to a window as he marvelled at the breathtaking panoramic view of the surrounding country.

Travelling through a wild reserve, he saw reticulated giraffes, gravy zebras, and wildebeest, among other wild grazing animals, moving around the parched dry land, dusting the dry ground with their hooves as if that would expose some pasture hidden in the ground.

Many had succumbed to the drought and lay surrounded by swarms of vultures, marabou storks and other scavengers who were having a field day feasting on the carcasses.

Occasionally, a hyena would make the famous laugh as it approached the birds. They would take a noisy and reluctant flight only to land a few metres from the carcass and wait impatiently for the hyena to have its fill and leave before descending on what remained of the carcass.

He recalled that his grandmother once told him that "the hyena made the mischievous laugh as a signal call to other hyenas," - informing them of a kill or a carcass.

He also saw thorn trees, red cedar and occasionally the famous baobabs with their large trunks. He once heard his grandfather say that, when travelling through a park in their youth, they would quench their thirst by drinking water caught in the hollows of the large branches.

They would also roast its seeds to make a coffee-like beverage. He said its trunk could hold 100,000 litres of water, of which nomads would make use when there was drought in the countryside. He wondered to himself how some travelling nomad would know that there in the expansive dry park, was an oasis in the form of a baobab.

They continued with their journey into the African wilderness as day turned into night.

***

The government finally admitted that there was famine in the country due to the prolonged drought and that the national grain reserve was finally running out. It appealed for international aid.

The media and the back bench in parliament did not waste time to remind the government that, as drought was a natural disaster, famine was man-made because it could be avoided if the government had made adequate plans, like building dams in drought prone regions, buying enough grain from farmers and taking other rafts of measures.

And predictably, just like they do every year, Oxfam, the Red Cross and other relief agencies took up the relief effort and called for the international community to assist in funding the efforts to avert a looming disaster.

Waciuri finally arrived in the coastal town at night. The following day, he took a dhow ride to the island of Mula and was fascinated by the coastal town. The streets were narrow, cool and quiet and there were no vehicles in sight.

The usual mode of transport was by donkey in the surprisingly intimate spaces between white washed buildings built with coral many centuries ago. These were perfectly woven around a Swahili theme, which gave the town its distinct colour and texture.

The town was protected from the ocean by coral reefs and large sand dunes. He had never seen such a massive mass of water; the most he had seen were the lakes and rivers back in the village.

As he was going to the port to meet James, he could see the bazaars in the market square where life seemed to move at a slow pace, unlike in Rukuna. The locals here had a relaxed and welcoming attitude.

Along the roadside, women dressed in *kangas* (wrappers) sold an array of snacks, which included *mshikaki* (meat on skewers), coconut milk, *samosas* (stuffed pastry) and *mahamri* (spiced doughnut).

The aromas which filled the air were inviting and he was tempted to stop and grab a snack when he quickly remembered that he had a job at hand. He hurriedly went towards the port after asking for directions.

"Yes, I have been expecting someone from the city. What did you come to look for in this sleepy coastal town," James asked Waciuri when they got acquainted.

"I'm looking for stock fish to take back to the city," Waciuri answered back as he had been instructed.

James was one of the many in the underground network who worked to help those that were pressing the government on reforms. He was an important link between them and MacClare, the Minister for Trade.

The question that he asked Waciuri was meant to ensure that he was talking to the right person and not to a government mole. One could not be too sure nowadays.

Waciuri then provided the address of Njoroge's business premises where some deliveries were to be made in the coming days.

He decided to spend a few days in the coastal town to explore the beautiful part of this country before heading back to the village.

Chapter Fifteen

The crackdown on dissidents intensified throughout the country, and many people would find themselves at the State Research Bureau where they would confess to accusations about which they did not know anything just to stop the tortures.

Kamangu's youth wingers would falsely accuse people they wanted to settle scores with. They would claim that they were anti-government and have them arrested and taken in by the Special Branch for questioning, many of them never to be seen again in the village.

**

It was a typical sunny afternoon, when Waciuri took a stroll towards one of the many isolated villages on his way to the pristine beaches, soaking the warmth in the breathtaking surroundings.

On his way, he found an old weary man sitting under a coconut tree to shield himself from the searing afternoon heat.

He realised that people were not paying any particular attention to him, and he seemed to have been around the neighbourhood for quite some time now. He decided to find out how the old man was doing and if he needed any assistance.

"Good afternoon sir, my name is Waciuri from back in the village. Can I help in anyway?" Waciuri and his age mates were always taught to respect and assist their elders back in the village.

"My young man, I'm both hungry and thirsty and no one has come up to ask me how I'm doing. Has the world come to this?" the old man replied.

"Anyway, what would kill me now is thirst. If I could only get a mug of water," he added.

"Not only will I get you water, but also something to eat to help you continue with your journey," Waciuri offered.

He suggested to him that it would be easier and faster if he went back to the market alone and get him some food as the old man looked obviously too tired to walk.

He could spare some money to buy the old man some fish, chapatti and coconut milk, which he got from the women selling food at the market square.

"May God bless you my son," the old man said after he had eaten. 'What brings you to Mula anyway? he enquired.

"I came to visit a friend before schools open. You can call it a holiday visit," Waciuri answered.

"My name is Karim Mohammed and my title is Mawlana- an Islamic clergy," the old man finally gave a name to his face.

"I have travelled the length and breadth of the earth from the Himalayas, to the Amazon and through the forests of Africa in search of the sacred river," he said.

"And how does the sacred river look like? The one that you seek?" Waciuri asked puzzled, as he had never heard about such a river even from the fables that his grandmother told him.

"The sacred river is the place where the arrow of God struck the earth and forth came a stream. Whoever finds the river is truly blessed, for whoever drinketh from it becomes whole and finds his true purpose in his life," Mohammed explained.

Waciuri looked him in the eyes and, for the first time, saw the wisdom in his eyes; that of a man who had seen a lot in the many years that he had lived.

"I'm on a pilgrimage in search of that elusive river and I have made it my duty to find it," Mohammed told him to break the silence that ensued.

"What is your purpose on this earth," he went on.

"What?" Waciuri asked. Not that he had not heard him, but that he had never thought about it before.

"I've never thought about it. My grandmother always tells me to read books so that I become someone big in the government," Waciuri tried to find an answer to that question.

"It is important to seek knowledge, but when God created you, he had a purpose for you. It is your duty to find out what your purpose is," Mohammed advised.

And there and then, Waciuri made a decision to stay with Mohammed for the few days he was in Mula. He had a lot to learn from the old man- the hermit.

***

In the port city of Rukuna, a freight ship was offloading maize that had been brought in by Oxfam to be distributed to areas that were hard hit by the famine.

The government and Oxfam had made an appeal to companies or individuals operating transport businesses to help in the distribution of the maize by offering transport services.

Many businessmen had used their political connections to win tenders for maize distribution, but a few who owned fleets of lorries had also managed to win some of the tenders. Things in the government were no longer transparent and the few that got the tenders without corrupting government officials got them only because Oxfam was part of the tendering group.

One of the few that got a share in the tender without involving corrupt government officials had two of its Bedford lorries parked at the offloading yard waiting to fill up.

The plan had been to make a detour once they filled up with relief food and go to a depot to collect goods that had come in the previous night by a dhow.

When the two lorries finally got to the depot, they found two other lorries with wooden crates marked- G.O.D (Government Of Donyokeri).

The relief maize was offloaded, the heavy wooden crates were loaded into the four lorries, and the relief maize was loaded back into all the lorries. The crates were now perfectly concealed by the maize.

The contraband had come from one of the states of the Soviet Union and had been brought in by an American contractor, after it had been sourced by those wishing to bring change in the country.

The goods were some of the many that were coming in from various points and were to be distributed to the various parts of the country.

Some of the lorries would find their way to Njoroge's charcoal yard before proceeding to Mutituini. Njoroge was one of the underground network agents who was fighting for the cause, and sometimes, tough times called for tough measures.

***

Juma and company had been holed up in the safe house for almost a week now in what seemed like eternity.

The first few days, they would venture out in the compound, which was surrounded with a hedge fence, but lately they were not venturing outside the house.

The informers, in the name of Youth Wingers, were now going round the village looking for those they suspected to be sympathizers of those asking for reforms. They could not therefore take any chances by spending their time outside the house.

They were following events on the radio whose volume was turned down low so as not to attract attention. If all went well, they would head to the nearby forest of Ol Donyo Mountain, where they would begin their campaign to force Sonkoh's government to reform.

Chapter Sixteen

Waciuri and his new found friend Mohammed were headed to the pristine sandy white beaches of Mula to spend some time there lazing on the beach and soaking in the warmth of that day.

"I marvelled the first time I saw the sea. The largest mass of water that I have ever seen is the lake in our village that is fed by the rivers originating from the mountain," Waciuri told Mohammed.

"The ocean occupies two thirds of our earth and the other third is land mass. If you were to travel by this sea, you would find yourself in foreign lands far away from your village," Mohammed explained.

"Yes! We learn about it in school in our geography class but I'm glad that I have seen it with my own eyes," Waciuri said.

When they got to the beach, lapped by clear turquoise waters, they found some boys diving from the pier to the sea, a steep drop indeed. And even though Waciuri knew how to swim, he could not attempt their antics. They had grown up doing this. Instead, he would swim from where the sea waves touched the shore.

"Go ahead, I'll wait for you here under the coconut tree as you go for a swim," Mohammed told him when he read his thoughts.

Waciuri dove into the warm salty waters with excitement. Unlike the cold fresh water of the lake and rivers that he was used to, the sea had a different feeling of life in it.

Mohammed removed his worn-out notebook that he always carried with him and started writing his diary, slowly, as he watched the activity around him.

***

When the lorries finally reached Mutituini, it was already dusk. Juma and his group went to meet them at the edge of the forest.

After offloading the wooden crates, the lorries resumed their journeys to distribute the relief food. Some of the relief maize would also be distributed around Mutituini village.

They hurriedly opened the crates at random to see if the equipment they wanted was all there.

Some of the crates held an assortment of assault rifles, most of them AK47's and a few submachine guns. Others had two-way communication tools like walkie-talkies, first aid kits and land mines.

"I'm glad that they got us the land mines. These will prove to be very useful in our campaign," Juma observed. Their plan was not to attack government soldiers but rather to target important installations like bridges, power lines and the like in order to bring the government to the negotiating table.

But at the back of his mind, he knew that a confrontation was inevitable and therefore the need to have weapons to defend themselves. "Better to be prepared than be sorry," he thought to himself.

"Sometimes, the price of liberty is earned through bloodshed as history has shown," the revolutionary Wafula said as he was running his hands around the cold metal barrel of an AK47 rifle.

They hurriedly carried the crates to a thicket before night time caught up with them and carried what they could up the mountain, where they would set up their camp away from the prying eyes of the Special Branch or the notorious youth wingers.

They would come for the rest of the goods later. It would probably take them another day or two before they could bring everything up to the camp that they intended to set up.

***

As the afternoon dragged on lazily, Waciuri had joined Mohammed to rest under the shade of the coconut tree. He had become exhausted from swimming in the flapping sea waves of the Indian Ocean.

"I was intending to find accommodation in town and I can only afford a single room, perhaps we can share it," Waciuri offered.

"If you go and stay in town, how then can you say you are on vacation? You should stay among the locals and learn their way of life," Mohammed replied.

"But I don't know anyone here, we are strangers and unlike back at home, there is no neighbour that I can ask for accommodation," Waciuri explained.

"Doesn't your Bible teach about the Good Samaritan? But let us first visit one of the villages and get acquainted with their way of life."

And so they started walking towards the mangrove forest. It started raining, first as a drizzle and then it poured in torrents even though the day was sunny. They took shelter in the mangroves until the short-lived rain disappeared just as it had come.

Although it had just finished raining, the air was hot, humid and close. Nobody else was in sight; the only sound, other than insects, the chirping of birds and sea gulls, was that of low crashing sea waves in the distance.

They continued with their journey to the interior until they came around an area covered by weeds and lianas, which parasitically clung onto trees in an effort to compete for sun rays above the forest floor.

Around them, on the sparsely covered white sand, was a scatter of stones: the outlines of a now vanished ancient building, revealed by archeologists many years ago.

And standing like a sentry by its entrance was a faded incomplete sign written in Arabic - Sultan H-

"This was an ancient kingdom of the Sultan of Oman, who came all the way by sea to the African coast and was so enchanted by the beauty of the virgin country that he decided to stay," Mohammed explained when he saw that Waciuri was puzzled with the ruins.

"What made them come into this country in the first place," Waciuri asked.

"They came with their ships to trade. They would barter their silk, spices and gold bracelets for slaves captured from the interior," Mohammed proffered.

"That is how Africans ended up in other continents like Asia and the Americas. They initially went there as slaves and ended up as free citizens of those countries after the abolition of the slave trade," he went on.

After lingering in the ruins for a while, to let the lessons that he had just received from the religious man sink, they went on with their journey.

***

Somewhere in front, they could hear a river gurgling. In the darkness, the water was hardly visible, but one could feel and almost smell its violence.

"This is just a stream but when it rains, we could be in trouble. It's better to be careful. Give me a machete somebody," Bildad, who had assumed the role of a guide, said. When he was growing up, he used to come to this forest. He used to lead boys for deer hunting back in the days.

In the pitch darkness of the forest, Juma passed him a machete, and he used it to cut off a tall bamboo stick from a clump on the bank.

They crossed the swollen stream, Bildad leading with his stick, testing the depth of the water. Everybody was silent and only their panting could be heard.

This part of the forest they were using was a trail for elephants and buffaloes, but they walked on without mishap and finally came to a glade which had a cave nearby. All the memories came flashing back when Bildad recalled when they used to come here and roast the deer meat in the clearing.

That is where they set camp. They were all exhausted from the climbing and from carrying the wooden crates. Tomorrow, they would go down and collect the remaining crates before starting their campaign. It was rumoured that other regions had already started their sabotage and it was only a matter of time before Sonkoh's government would call for a ceasefire, or so they thought.

They lit a bonfire from the dead twigs and other tinder that Muthoni had collected from around the camp to keep themselves warm and also to keep wild animals away as they slept.

They cooked dinner and ate as they strategized for the days ahead.

Chapter Seventeen

It was late in the afternoon when finally Waciuri and Mohammed came across one village in a clearing in the forest.

It was an idyllic village with huts thatched with *makuti* (coconut tree fronds). The compounds around the huts were thoroughly swept. They were so clean they looked like a cement floors.

Even before they got to the village, children ran to meet them as it was obvious that they were visitors. It had been a while since anyone from outside their community had come to visit.

"Welcome to our village. We always look forward to visitors because they always come with good tidings," the village elder greeted them as he summoned them to sit on the wooden stools that were brought out by bare chested young Giriama girls.

"Thank you," they both replied in unison. They explained that they were local tourists visiting the coastal town. For Waciuri, it felt like home sitting in his grandmother's kitchen when he sat on the wooden stools that they were offered.

"We cannot allow you to travel at night. The least we can do is let you stay for the night or until whenever you want to leave, feel at home," the elder, whose hair was pure white with age, told them with a smile on his face.

"Thank you, we are going to stay for the night but will be on our way tomorrow. Thank you once again for your hospitality and may God bless you," Mohammed replied.

Dinner was served on a big tray made of *makuti* (coconut fronds). They all sat and ate fish and *ugali* (grain meal) made from millet accompanied by chili peppers and spicy potatoes. They would pick the *ugali,* mould it to a

81

ball, dip it in the fish sauce and bring it up into their waiting open mouths and gobble it. This is how they ate from the large tray. It strengthened their communal bond.

When finally they all retired to their huts, Mohammed lit the oil lamp that used coconut oil as fuel and began to teach Waciuri the meaning of the parable of the Good Samaritan.

"When you told me earlier that there wasn't a neighbour in this town, you raised an important question. Who is your neighbour?" Mohammed asked Waciuri.

"A neighbour is a friend or someone you know," Waciuri replied.

"Not necessarily," and Mohammed used the parable of the Good Samaritan to explain.

"Jesus taught in your Bible who a good neighbour is," He went on. "This is the story of a Jewish traveler who was robbed and left for dead. A priest saw the man and crossed over to the other side of the road, presumably in order to maintain ritual purity. A Levite also ignored the half-dead traveller. Finally, a passing Samaritan, filled with compassion, stopped, gave assistance and offered to cover the expenses at a local inn for the man he had rescued."

He went on to explain that, as would have been expected, the priest and the Levite were the ones who should have stopped to help one of their own, more so for being religious leaders. Ironically, it was a Samaritan, though despised by the Jews, who offered to help.

"And so my young man, these strangers, just like yourself, who offered us their hospitality are the true neighbours," Mohammed explained as he finished. That for Waciuri was a great revelation and he resolved to call Mohammed- 'Master' or 'Teacher.'

They slept on the reed beds hanging from the rafters, soaking in the warmth of the African night and the music of chirping crickets. Waciuri dreamt of sailing on a dhow to unknown foreign lands of smiling avatars.

***

The night was very cold as Juma and his group crept along the bridge that connected Mutituini and the provincial headquarters, - Kiambiu.

It was a dark night and even though people in the village were asleep, they did not take their chances. They crept discreetly under the bridge and planted two mines on each end of the bridge. The mines were connected by some cables.

Juma swung his hand to look at his wrist watch using a flashlight. It was some minutes to midnight. He then gave his signal.

Wafula connected the cables, and the bridge blew up with a thunderous bang that lit the whole area for a moment. They saw birds that had retired to their nests in the trees take off in fright.

The sound must have travelled a long distance and so they hurriedly retreated to Mutituini market. On their way back, they set ablaze a green Land Rover, the only one in the village that was used for official duties. It was parked at the local DDP office. As well, they set, poles of power lines on fire before retreating back to the safety of the forest.

Dogs started howling in the night because of the disturbances and villagers came out to find out what was happening.

As expected, there a major blackout when the power lines short-circuited when they fell on each other after the poles had burnt out. Villagers had to use torches to move around.

When they came to douse the burning car, it was too late and their efforts were in vain for the car had completely burnt out into a shell. They were bewildered because they had never encountered such an occurrence before.

The village had been relatively safe before. They eventually left for their homes while talking in hushed tones with hands on their chins and shaking their heads.

The following day an impromptu meeting was convened by Bwana Kamangu, the local administrator and the local security team, after a drummer went around the village beating his drum to catch the attention of the villagers as he made the announcement of the unexpected meeting.

Word had by now gone around, thanks to the media, that people affiliated with the PDA had, through attacks on key government infrastructures began a campaign to force the government to allow for elections and to respect human rights such as the freedom of assembly and speech.

"I don't need to remind you of what took place last night," Bwana Kamangu spoke when he opened the meeting.

"We have reliable information that the attacks that took place were perpetrated by people among you; people in this community who have decided to take the law into their hands," he continued.

"Be prepared to meet the full force of the law unless you give up those vandals that you are habouring," he went on. People began to murmur in disapproval and whisper furtively among themselves.

"You cannot heap blame on the whole community because of the acts of a few," one elderly man who was an elder in the community finally pointed out.

"Isn't the duty of your government to ensure that we have security? But arresting innocent youth like the way your youth wingers have been doing is not helping matters, it is only creating resentment and animosity," another elderly woman said feebly.

"Then you all know what needs to be done. Give us the whereabouts of Juma and his gang or be prepared to do so when the government sends its troops here to mop up the rebels. I promise you, you won't like it then," Bwana Kamangu warned them.

Chapter Eighteen

President Sonkoh was livid when he spoke in the security meeting that he had urgently called for. The security chiefs listened timidly as he ranted.

"What is this nonsense I'm hearing of illiterate peasants going around causing havoc as if there is no government?" President Sonkoh bellowed.

"What are you people doing about it? Are you people paid to sleep on your job?" he went on.

"It's only a pocket of disturbances in a few places that we are going to contain in a matter of days, your Excellency," the head of Special Branch pointed out.

"Are our jails so full that you cannot arrest any more lawbreakers?" the president continued.

"In fact, my men are..." – the head of Special Branch was about to say when Ngei, the Minister for Defence and Home Affairs, cut him short.

"Your Excellency, these are not ordinary criminals but rebels who want to undermine or, worse still, try to overthrow a duly elected government," Minister Ngei said.

"We should engage them on a level equal to the threat posed; what I want to say, is that we should involve the military," he went on.

"Don't you think you are getting ahead of yourself, Ngei? This is just a small altercation by a few disgruntled peasants without any military training," the commissioner of police cut in.

"Do what you have to; all I want is to have this uprising crushed once and for all. We must show them who is in charge here," the president finally ordered.

The meeting would continue in that direction, and the president assured them that they had his blessings in carrying out their work.

In the meantime, the head of special branch went to see the president off so as to get an opportunity to update him on the progress of his mission. He had previously asked the president for permission to bug into the phones of those in the security committee because he felt there was a mole among them, and the president had given his consent.

***

The following morning, Waciuri woke up when streaks of sunrays broke through the thatch roof of the hut, lighting the room dimly and dappling his body. He was surprised to see that Master was not there.

He jumped out of his bed and went out rubbing his groggy red eyes to adjust to the morning brightness. He finally saw him seated with the village elder, drinking herbal tea as they chatted.

"Good morning my young man, I can see you finally woke up. You slept like a log last night," Mohammed greeted Waciuri.

"Good morning both of you, I dreamt that I had traveled to faraway lands and I guess I lost track of time," Waciuri said as he greeted back, suppressing a tired yawn.

After they had taken breakfast of herbal tea and cassava, it was time to go and every member of that clan was outside to bid them farewell.

The naked young boys oblivious of their nakedness, the topless young girls whose breasts had just started forming as small bumps, the women with their beautifully decorated *kangas* (wrappers) and a few men with wrappers covering their waist downwards were all there to bid them goodbye.

They thanked them profusely for their hospitality and left for Mula town, trekking through the mangrove forest where sun rays leaked through the thick foliage above, producing a luminous array of bright colours.

"I know that we have not spent much time together on this exotic island but remember that I have a mission of finding the sacred river, and I will not find it by staying on this island. I have to keep going," Mohammed said as they walked towards Mula town.

"I know, perhaps I can join you in your search," Waciuri pointed out.

"I have to travel by foot, if I travel by train or vehicle I might just pass the river without knowing. You need to travel back to your village after your vacation here, and in any case, you would tire if you chose to walk with me rather than taking the train," Mohammed observed.

"I have decided to walk to the city Rukuna and perhaps I can help you locate the sacred river," Waciuri confidently replied. He very much wanted to see how this river looked like. The other reason was that he also wanted to find out his purpose in life.

Mohammed was not sure about the whole idea, but they continued walking towards Mula town each engrossed in his own thoughts.

When they finally got to Mula town, the sun was searing hot above the cloudless sky. They walked the winding narrow streets towards the market bazaar where they sat down in one of the many open eateries to have lunch.

As they were taking *pilau* (spiced rice) and shark soup, they heard people talking animatedly about the recent uprising in the country. It had now become a topical issue in major towns.

"Do they think they can take on the government? We are all oppressed but the best we can do is ask the Holy Spirit to touch our leaders so that they can remember those who elected them," one person was heard saying.

"They are just idle people with nothing better to do. Do they now think they are more manly than the rest of us?" another one said.

Mohammed took that opportunity to address them and told them that there were better ways of opposing the government, like holding peaceful demonstrations throughout the country, if only they had organised visionary leaders to guide them.

"They will not hesitate to shoot the demonstrators, they will not think twice about it; they are ruthless," one person told Mohammed.

"They cannot shoot all of us, their conscience will prick their hearts at some point and give in to the demands of the masses," Mohammed told them. He wanted to tell them about Martin Luther King Jr. and Mahatma Gandhi but he was not sure they would understand the comparison.

He instead told them that those who live by the sword will die by the sword and that violence breeds more violence.

When they had taken their fill, they took a dhow and travelled to the mainland where they would begin their trek into the hinterland of the country in search of the sacred river.

An hour later, without warning, the floor of the ocean seemed to rise and a mountainous black body, dripping with foam, heaved upwards over their heads. It paused an instant, then fell sideways to be swallowed up by a vortex of green water.

If it had fallen their way, the dhow would have been crushed beneath its hundred and fifty tons.

They were dumbfounded when they saw the blue whale burst from the water for an instant. How could they adequately communicate the impact of something that immense?

Chapter Nineteen

The mechanised unit of the Donyokeri Armed Forces moved steadily on their way to Mutituini, their tanks spewing black smoke. The convoy of army trucks behind them led by Major Ruheni in the operation code-named, - Operation Mallet.

When they got to the point where the bridge had been blown up by Juma and his group, the mechanised unit began constructing a temporary bridge.

Major Ruheni took the hiatus of the journey to look at the distant village with the infra-red binoculars, while the soldiers came out of the Mercedes trucks using the sturdy sisal ropes tied behind the trucks,- to stretch their tired legs from much sitting.

Looking through the lenses, he could see hamlets dotted in the background of the pink image that the infra-red binoculars produced.

He could also smell the sickly odour of cannabis smoke drifting in the cold air from the joints that his men sat smoking on the side of the road. Though smoking weed was prohibited, it was overlooked in certain circumstances, and this was one of those.

After one hour, the temporary steel bridge that the tanks had carried lay across the river and the battalion proceeded with the journey.

Meanwhile, the village had long gone to sleep, oblivious of the activity that was unfolding. Only the rhythmic music of the crickets interrupted the quiet night.

When Major Ruheni's men got near the village, they switched off their engines and hurriedly moved stealthily the remainder of the journey, with their assault rifles slung on their shoulders.

And then the dogs began barking. Young men came out with *simis* (swords) to defend their homes only to be met with rifles pointed at them and told to lie down. Those that resisted were summarily shot dead.

Other soldiers kicked the doors open, with their boots, looking for young men only to be met with the startled, scared, screaming faces of those they found inside. Suddenly, any young man had become the enemy.

A soldier entered one particular hut, raised his rifle and pointed its muzzle on the head of one startled man shaken out of his deep sleep by the noise of his now shattered door and too scared to utter any word.

"So you think you can fight us you untrained rebel," the soldier barked at the now speechless lad before pulling the trigger. The room was splattered with white matter and bright red blood which was spurting from what remained of his head. He had always wanted to do this and it strangely made him aroused; he now felt like a true soldier.

Others women -- mothers and young girls -- they dragged them to the bushes and gang raped them. The young men who were rounded up were taken to a field for further interrogation.

Blood flowed copiously from the dead, now littered in their huts, creating rivulets of dark blood which seeped into the thirsty, dry earth.

Terror-ridden screams of the villagers filled the cold air of that fateful night as those young men who had managed to escape the onslaught ran towards the forest.

***

Waciuri disembarked from the dhow and bought the two gourds that Mohammed had told him would be useful in their long trek.

"We need to have gourds for carrying water to drink. Do you know that what kills a hungry and thirsty person is not lack of food? When your body lacks water, the metabolism activity in your body shuts down, affecting the major organs of your body," Mohammed had told him.

And so when they began their journey into the hinterland, they had water gourds strapped to their waists. These bobbed with the movement of their legs.

"How will you know that the river that you seek is the sacred river?" Waciuri asked him as they walked.

"When I see it I will know that it's the river that I have always sought. It will be a *déjà vu* moment, like it's something I had dreamt about before," Mohammed told him.

"Have you ever had a *déjà vu* moment in your life?" he continued.

"Yes! I once dreamt that visitors had come into our home to buy chicken from me and some days later, a neighbour did indeed come into our compound to buy some guinea fowls I had trapped near a river bank, and I recalled the dream," Waciuri remembered.

"All the same, we will ask locals the names of the big rivers that we come across," Mohammed told him.

And so they walked for several days through the dry country, passing through arid thorn-studded plains and through dry seasonal river beds, marvelling at the beautiful country.

One day, they met two tall, lean, dark skinned girls with wrappers tied around their mid-sections and nothing else, balancing earthen pots on their heads and walking leisurely, chatting among themselves.

They had beaded jewellry on their bare chests and anklets tied around their legs. Their skins glinted from their sweat which was reflecting the hot sun rays, as they strutted bare-footed towards the river.

"Hallo!" Mohammed greeted them. "I can see you are going to the river to fetch some water. Perhaps you can tell us the name of the river," he went on.

They told him the name of the river, which had not dried out owing to its large size. It was fed by other seasonal rivers and one could see the huge smooth boulders jutting out where the waters had receded.

"Why does he ask?" one of the girls with shapely, feminine legs and feet, asked Waciuri.

"Ask what?" Waciuri asked back.

"The name of the river," she went on.

"My Master is searching for the sacred river that came forth when the arrow of God struck and a stream came forth," Waciuri explained.

Both girls burst into fits of laughter before asking if the old man was crazy. Waciuri told them in jest that most of the time he wasn't crazy but only when enquiring about the sacred river, to which they continued laughing. Mohammed joined in their amusement when his face broke into a big smile.

"But perhaps you can refill our gourds with water," Waciuri pointed out. One of the girls with ebony skin squatted on the bank of the river and, using a half cut gourd, scooped water from the river and poured it into their empty gourds.

They would later use the same method to fill their earthen pots, before they all headed back to their village as the orange glare of the setting sun reflected on the lustrous landscape.

When they got to the homestead, the smouldering golden orb finally sank behind the distant horizon.

The homestead was surrounded by a hedge fence of dry thorn branches that deterred wild animals from sneaking in and snatching their cattle and goats at night.

In the compound, there were several *manyattas*

(small houses) that were built by their womenfolk by folding branches into an igloo-like shape, only stretched longer, forming an oblong shaped house. The frame was packed with leaves and plastered all over with cow dung, which acted as a deterrent to termites. The entrance to the house was small and one had to bend over to enter.

While the women built manyattas, cooked and fetched water and the young men herded cattle and protected the community from cattle-rustlers, the old men usually sat down under the shade of a tree to discuss bridal price and arbitrate on issues brought to them while brushing their teeth with a natural tooth brush.

The toothbrush came from branches of a certain tree that was cut into candle-sized length. One end was chewed to make a brush. They used the brushed end to brush their teeth in an anticlockwise motion, and the bark of the stick would produce natural toothpaste.

Once the paste wore off, they bit off the brush and chewed again to form a new toothbrush. This process would go on until the stick was reduced in size gradually like a burning candle. Their teeth were usually milk-white because of this natural toothbrush.

This is the kind of homestead that Waciuri and Mohammed entered that evening. They were received by the patriarch of the compound.

"Good evening sir, we are on a pilgrimage and were hoping that we could sleep overnight in your homestead even if it means paying you for lodging us," Mohammed said after greeting the old man.

"God forbid! We do not charge travelers who lodge with us, we are a nomadic community and we move a lot in search of pasture. And when it gets late, we usually lodge in the nearest homestead for free," the old man of the homestead replied back as he welcomed them.

After having taken a hot meal that was served to them, they retreated into a *manyatta* that was vacated to make room for them. Mohammed used the tin lamp beside the reed bed to write notes in his dog-eared smeared notebook, and Waciuri wondered what he often wrote about in that notebook before sleep got the better of him.

The following day, their gourds were filled with fermented milk that had a sour-tart; slightly bitter taste after the inside of the gourd that was used to ferment the milk was first rubbed with a smoking stick of *Olea Africana,* the tree that gave the milk its distinctive taste.

They were also given strips of dry, smoked goat meat as they bade them goodbye. The milk would later prove to be very useful in energizing them during their long journey.

***

The following day, Mutituini village looked liked a war zone. Wailing filled the air after the massacre that had taken place the previous night became obvious. Even villagers couldn't go to console each other as most homes had been bereaved.

Major Ruheni's men had set camp a mile away from the village. This is where they undertook ruthless interrogation of the young men they had arrested the previous night. Those that succumbed were buried in shallow graves to conceal the atrocities that were taking place and those that were released were warned with dire consequences if they spoke to the media about what they had witnessed.

Those that had run to the safety of the welcoming arms of the forest finally hooked up with Juma's group and told them of the atrocities that had taken place back in the village. Some blamed Juma and his team for what had taken place.

"Playing the blame game will not solve anything," Juma told them. "That is what the soldiers would like to happen. We need to stand united to fight this aggression that has visited us,'" he went on.

"Are we going to fight with our bare hands!" one of the young men with a creased brow asked sneeringly.

"We don't have much, but we are surely not going to fight with our bare hands," Juma told them. He asked Bildad and Wafula to show them the arsenal that they had with them.

He would later divide the hundred or so young men into units. Some were given guns, others were tasked with laying down mines after they were given a crash course by the revolutionary Wafula, while others would act as scouts.

Juma would later tell Muthoni that they did not need to recruit young men as the action of the soldiers had created a pool of angry vengeful men for them.

He warned his small band of men that it was only a matter of time before the soldiers carried out an operation to flush them out from the forest and ordered that land mines be laid at the edge of the forest to slow them down.

He would later relay news of the massacre that had taken place with their communication gadgets to anyone who cared to listen, and their signal was picked up by the media.

Chapter Twenty

After the news of the massacre came out, there was uproar from the international community. Sonkoh's government tried to down play the aggression that it was employing to fight the uprising.

Ambassadors from sympathetic countries gathered to explain their government's displeasure and to deliver protest notes to Sonkoh's government.

***

As the army truck was coming to drop a detachment of soldiers near the edge of the forest, some young men sprung out from a nearby brush and sprayed the windscreen with a hail of bullets. The truck went out of control and landed in a ditch. The driver lay slumped over the steering wheel.

Soldiers began to jump out of the truck. The men behind the brushwood continued to fire in a frenzy and two soldiers fell under a hail of bullets.

The rebels then retreated as the soldiers tactically took cover and started shooting towards the brush that was spewing bullets. They moved forward cautiously, just like they had been trained, ducking from the intermittent crackling sound of gunfire coming from the now retreating rebels.

The soldiers were gaining ground. But this was a trap that they were being lured into because as soon as they got to the edge of the forest, the landmines began to go off, hurling a dozen of the soldiers up in the air like rag-dolls.

The commander called for a tactical retreat and called Major Ruheni to inform him about the sudden change of circumstances. Major Ruheni called back his team. He had not expected this kind of resistance and did not expect that the rebels they came to subdue were equally armed. He relayed this to his superiors back in the city for further instructions.

***

Mumbi had gone to almost all the police stations in Rukuna to enquire on the whereabouts of Juma.

She would go to the reporting desk of a police station that was manned by two angry and lethargic looking police officers, normally a male and female officer, and ask if they had Juma in their custody.

"Aahmm - excuse me, I'm looking for a Mr. Juma who was arrested and was wondering if he is in your custody?" Mumbi would ask timidly in any of the many police stations she visited.

"Madam! Do you know how many Jumas there are in Donyokeri?" a male officer would ask her in an intimidating manner.

"Ah... Shujaa Juma," she would give them both his names. "What is his crime?" the lady officer would chip in. "I don't know, he was arrested in Mutituini and brought to the city because of holding a meeting," Mumbi would try to explain the circumstances that led to his arrest.

The angry-looking male police officer would then run his index finger slowly through the Occurrence Book (OB) to see if Juma was one of the suspects booked in that police station before shaking his head to indicate that he was not there.

It was only after she went to one particular police station, where she met a genial, motherly police woman, that she got some information. After asking what Juma was arrested for and her relationship with him, the policewoman told her that he was probably a political
100

prisoner and that she would not find him in any of the police stations.

"You will probably never see him again; concentrate on your studies young woman. You have a long future ahead of you and you will meet someone else along the way," the police woman advised her.

When she heard the words that she had always dreaded hearing, she went out of the police station with a feeling of dejection and utter hopelessness.

***

Waciuri and Mohammed continued with their journey, inching closer to Rukuna, the capital city of Donyokeri. They had not discovered the sacred river yet, and Waciuri's little money that he was given for his fare back from Mula had already dwindled out.

Fortunately, they had found kind locals on their long trek who not only had hosted them, but also had provided them with food and drink. This went to affirm what Mohammed had told him that, one's neighbour was not necessarily someone you knew, but that even a stranger could be more than a neighbour; perhaps closer than a brother.

And these acts of random kindness went on to prove to him that there was something inherently virtuous in every human being.

One day, as they were walking through a wilderness, they passed by an area that had acacia thorn trees and overgrown dry bushes. Suddenly, a rapid movement in the bush drew their attention to the undergrowth.

Then they saw it. A rouge male buffalo that had probably been chased from the herd by other younger males that wanted to take his position as the Alpha Male. It stood there, staring suspiciously at them with blood-shot eyes.

They stood transfixed on the spot staring back at the buffalo. The world stood silent and still, as if lost for a moment in time as they gazed in muted distress. And the buffalo flicked his ears, as if telling them to say their final prayers before it charged at them.

And after what seemed like an eternity, Mohammed finally whispered that they should retreat by moonwalking backwards while still facing the buffalo. After moving this way for a considerable distance, they took to their heels. The buffalo watched them with bemusement, unsure about whether to chase after them or not.

After running for several minutes and being completely out of sight from the buffalo, they finally came to a stop, panting breathlessly. Their hearts felt as if they were on fire and would explode out of their chests any moment as they stooped and put their hands on their knees to take a breath.

They later rested their tired limbs when they sat leaning their backs on an anthill in the savannah.

Another day, while on their long trek, they came across a stream and were about to step on the smooth stones to cross over to the other side of the river bank when suddenly Waciuri saw a King Cobra nearby with its raised hooded head staring at them.

"Look! A Cobra snake!" Waciuri screamed in alarm. Mohammed stared at the cobra calmly before crossing over the stream politely. The King Cobra followed his movements mechanically with its head.

"Learn to overcome the fear within you and cross the stream calmly by taking long breaths" Mohammed told him. Waciuri was not sure about this but after some considerable time, he gathered all the courage he could muster and crossed the stream, trembling as the King Cobra observed him just as it had done with Mohammed.

And for a moment, Waciuri thought that perhaps Mohammed was not only a holy man, but that he could also perform miracles.

Today, they sat under a Baobab tree, resting in its shade, and Mohammed was telling Waciuri anecdotal stories as they savoured the beauty of the surrounding area. Without warning, an African Eagle Owl suddenly spread its wings and flew off from a tall slender Nandi Flame tree in bloom with crimson bell-shaped flowers.

"Is the sighting of an owl a sign of bad omen...like death?" Waciuri asked Mohammed suddenly, just like the way the owl had suddenly taken off.

They had not seen the owl earlier because it was camouflaged by the crimson bell-shaped flowers of the Nandi Flame tree.

"Owls are nocturnal creatures, which disturb the peace of dayfolks with their derisive hoots at night. Perhaps that's why people wrongly think that they are harbingers of doom. They however have their role to play in our ecosystem," Mohammed told him.

And he went on to explain that when death calls, no one can escape it, with or without the sighting of an owl. He underlined it all with the following anecdotal story, titled, - *A Date With Destiny*.

"Dimitrios was a business mogul with vast interests in oil, shipping and the steel industry. His chauffer was driving him to the Ritz Hotel in New York where he was to meet a businessman he had been chasing to close a business deal that would expand his business empire. Amassing wealth gave him a sense of security, after climbing his way up from the trenches."

When they got to the kerb of the Ritz, the chauffer walked to his side to open the door for him. He got out of his limousine and was walking pompously towards the revolving doors of the hotel, when he bumped into a vagrant, almost knocking him down. The vagrant's face was covered with a dirty smeared trench coat.

"He had an urgent appointment and did not apologise. He looked furtively at the poor man's face with arrogance because of the inconvenience."

What he saw shocked him! For he saw the face of Death; the face of the Grim Reaper.

"How did the face of death look like," Waciuri cut him short with curiosity mixed with excitement.

"Well, the face of the Grim Reaper has no flesh on it, only the skull," Mohammed told him as he went on with his story."

"The mogul turned back to look again, but the Grim Reaper had disappeared. He abandoned his appointment and went back hurriedly to his limousine and ordered his chauffer to drive him to the airport immediately."

"When he got there, he booked a flight for Nepal. Reaching Nepal the following day, he took a bus that drove him to Mt. Everest. When he got there, he bought rations and whatever else he needed to survive the cold of the summit and, with the help of local mountain climbers, he went to the top of the mountain and found himself a cave."

"He was now as far away as possible from Death, but taking no chances, he instructed the guides to erect tents near the cave and take sentry positions."

"In the evening, as he was taking a steamy meal of mountain goat soup, he thought he heard some movements and called out 'who's there,' thinking that perhaps it was one of the guides who had come to check on him."

When he looked up, it was the Grim Reaper himself. He crouched into a foetal position, bringing his hands to his knees in mortal fear as if that would save him from death.

'You know, when I met you in New York the other day, I knew we had an appointment at this very cave. But I would have bet with my life that you wouldn't honour it,' the Grim Reaper told him.

"But now that you have made it, you are dead on time,' Death continued, as he hovered towards the mogul. He screamed his heart out. 'Nooo! Noo...pleeeease' but his screams echoed back at him as if to mock him inside the dimlit cave."

From that story, Waciuri understood that with death, you can run but you cannot hide and it arrives punctually by appointment.

After a while, Mohammed took a siesta and Waciuri took that opportunity to pick the dog-eared smeared note book that laid on his chest and peek to see what his Master always wrote about. Curiosity had gotten the better of him.

He opened the notebook with anticipation, but his expectations dissipated when he realised that he could not read the extremely small hand writing that Mohammed used and that he would probably need a magnifying glass to read the contents of the note book.

Chapter Twenty One

The government had sent two geologists to Ol Donyokeri Mountain to prospect for minerals. The two Caucasians had quickly built a cabin near the mountain, where they stayed and kept their equipments.

Meanwhile, after the surprise resistance that Ruheni's soldiers met when they attempted to raid the forest and flush out the rebels, they took their anger out on the villagers, especially those whose sons had fled to the mountains.

They would go to homes and harass the relatives of those young men, enquiring about their profiles, like their age. If they had pictures taken of themselves, they got them after ransacking the homestead. They would also look to see if perhaps, they had left their ID's in their haste to flee to the safety of the forest.

They collected every document they could lay their hands on and took everything with them.

Bildad's workers at the wholesale shop were beaten up rather badly by the soldiers when they went there to ask about the whereabouts of their boss.

"Please officers, we don't know where Bildad went after the operation to arrest people in the village. Spare us this violence, have mercy on us," Bildad's wife pleaded as they beat up the workers with rifle butts.

"We are going to take you in for interrogation, perhaps then you will be able to produce your husband," one soldier, with a scar running between his eyes all the way down to his chin, barked at her.

"Please, I beg you. In the name of Christ, I don't know where my husband is," she pleaded with them.

"In fact you are wasting our energy, are we going to eat your pleas?" the soldier went on.

Then the soldiers entered the shop and helped themselves to foodstuffs and the day's sales kept in the till.

"Today, is your lucky day, but the next time we come back, we will go with you if you don't produce your husband," the soldier with the scar barked at her as they left, leaving one of her workers lying on the ground from the beatings.

Other soldiers entered Waciuri's homestead and asked the old folks for their grandson. They were given the list of villagers who were AWOL by the youth wingers.

"Where is your grandson? Is he in the forest?" one soldier snarled at Waciuri's grandfather when they found him and his wife basking in their compound.

"He left for Rukuna with friends about a month ago," Waciuri's grandmother replied. Meanwhile the other soldiers were ransacking the house, turning everything upside down and breaking earthen pots in the process.

"Why do you harass old people instead of picking on your age mates? Don't you see you are young enough to be my grand children?" Waciuri's grandfather wondered aloud in anger.

Their leader, who was smoking a roll of weed, dropped the smouldering butt and slowly squeezed it with his shiny black boots before descending on the old man with blows. The others took cue and joined him.

Waciuri's grandmother screamed as she begged them to leave her husband alone. They later did and left him writhing in pain. "Let me call the neighbours, we take you to the dispensary," Waciuri's grandmother told her husband when the soldiers had finally left.

"There's no need of disturbing our neighbours, just apply the bulbous plant that is normally placed on bruises after putting it near a fire to heat it," Waciuri's grandfather replied labouriously while wincing in pain.

And with that, Waciuri's grandmother went out to look for the fat leaves of the bulbous plant that was related to the cactus, all the while, cursing the soldiers for the abominable sin of beating up an old person.

***

Juma and his group were now resting after doing the morning drills. This was done to keep the young men in shape and to instill discipline in them.

They were cooking lunch to help them beat the extreme cold weather of the mountain when they heard the dull drone of an aeroplane far ahead. They wondered about it, because planes were not frequent visitors in that part of the country but shrugged it off and continued with their cooking.

They were not entirely dependent on canned food, because sometimes, the forest would feed them when they trapped small animals like deer and warthogs.

One day, Bildad and a scout went in search of honey and were amazed when a small bright coloured bird flew in front of them making strange signals by fluttering its wings. It led them for a considerable distance to a place with a huge log filled with a swarm of honey bees.

The bird was feeding on the honey inside the log. After it flew off, they collected some dry leaves and lit them producing smoke which they used to chase away the bees before collecting the honey and taking it back to their base to share with the rest of the group.

The dull drone of the plane now seemed closer and they thought that it was perhaps on a reconnaissance mission when without warning, the bird started laying its eggs.

The ground shook and pulsated as everyone started running for cover. The falling bombs created large craters on the ground. They also created casualties.

Muthoni had thrown herself next to Juma and pushed herself against him as if that could help shield her from the bombs. She clung tightly onto him as they lay on their stomachs on the ground.

After the madness had stopped, there was an eerie silence. Even the birds had stopped chirping. And Juma slowly raised his head and scanned around. Many people had not been so lucky; people he had chatted with a few minutes ago were now scattered pieces all over the place.

Wafula the revolutionary lay on his back side with a surprised look on his dead face, clutching a piece of shrapnel that went through his chest and exited from his back, not before shattering his backbone. Blood was also oozing from his open mouth.

They quickly took what they could and started running far away from their base, which now lay strewn with dead bodies. Apparently, the bomber had spotted the smoke that was rising above the mountain from their cooking fire.

Going through the forest, they met a herd of elephants which had been frightened and agitated by the noise of the exploding bombs. The herd chased them while trumpeting in anger. It was a bad day for all of them, and when they finally pitched tent in an area that was dotted with caverns, no one was talking to the other. The air was filled with a foul mood and despondence.

Juma talked to them in an effort to try and raise their spirits. "Obstacles will come, but always find a way to rise above those obstacles. We should stay together and united, at least we came out alive from this ordeal," he told them.

Later that evening, he would go to his cave and silently ponder about the events that had taken place earlier that day.

"The speech that you gave the group was very encouraging. Everything will be alright," Muthoni told him when she came to console him.

"Stay behind," Juma told her. And even though he had encouraged and talked tough with the young men, she saw in his eyes a look that did not really look like fear but... how could she put it, a look of weariness. A look of self doubt.

She held both his hands and she brought them to her face. He lowered one of his hands and touched her belly and kissed her closed lips before slipping his hand under her skirt.

She didn't stop him. He kissed her neck, her jaw, and her lips again before slipping his tongue into her now open mouth. The gushing warmth of it overwhelmed him.

He thought to himself how difficult it was to hold on to anything in the forest. There was no guarantee that one would live to see the following day. Nothing was yours, not even the right to give or withhold love as he held her and made love to her.

She clung to him and dug her nails into his back in the act of sweet love. "Have you ever loved anyone else?" she asked him the following morning when he woke up.

"No, the only person that I love is Mumbi and if I come out of here alive, I'll look for her," he replied. "I understand that," she replied, before giving him a warm hug.

***

When the news of the air raids that had been carried out in the mountains and forests of Donyokeri to flush out rebels came out, people took to the streets to protest all over the country like never before.

The police would be sent to clobber them with batons and lob tear gas canisters at them before engaging them in running battles to disperse them, but the following day they would regroup and come out in even larger numbers than the previous day.

The United Nations Security Council held an emergency meeting to pass a resolution for an air embargo on the skies of Donyokeri because of the deadly air raids, but The Soviet Union and China were opposed to it.

The hard tactics used by the armed forces against its own citizens began to divide the military, as some of the top brass felt that it was immoral for them, to carry out the same atrocities that the colonial government - they had fought hard against - committed against the peasantry.

Juma, who was now the unofficial leader and spokesman of the PDA, would release statements to the media from time to time from his hideout.

Chapter Twenty Two

Waciuri and Mohammed's long trek had finally brought them to Rukuna, the capital city of Donyokeri.

It had been a long and difficult trek so far and they were both weary and hungry. They still had not found the elusive sacred river and they had to continue with their pilgrimage.

They decided to take a respite at Uhuru Square before going on with their journey. "Let me go and find something to eat so that we can regain our strength before proceeding with our journey," Waciuri suggested to Mohammed.

And so Waciuri went to the city centre to see if he could get some food from good Samaritans. He got to an open air market in downtown Rukuna, where women were selling cooked food at some roadside eateries.

"Good afternoon mum, my Master and I have been on a long journey and the little money that we had is finished. I'm requesting for some food for my Master," Waciuri humbly begged one of the women.

"How do I know that you are not one of those delinquents roaming the streets? And who is your Master anyway?" the woman asked suspiciously.

"God is my witness that I'm not lying to you, my Master is a pious religious man I met in Mula," Waciuri answered.

"Anyway, let me give you some food for the mercy of God," the woman said before she gave Waciuri a generous serving of rice and beans. "My Master would not mind some soup," Waciuri said politely as he received the food.

"Hei! Does your Master eat like a horse now?" the woman asked while raising both her hands in the air and snapping her fingers. She then proceeded to add some goat soup and a morsel of goat meat for him.

"Thank you for your kindness, may God bless you," Waciuri profusely thanked the generous food vendor.

"Tell the man of God to pray for my daughter who is barren," the woman told Waciuri as he bade her farewell.

"I will do that," he replied as he left.

Later when they sat down to eat, Waciuri told him how he got the food and the woman's prayer request. Mohammed said a short prayer to bless the food and also asked God to meet the woman's wishes.

"This is a beautiful square where people come to rest their tired limbs and collect their thoughts in this urban jungle," Mohammed said, more to himself than in conversation after they had eaten and were now resting.

"It's a place of refuge of sorts. But this place will play a significant role in the future of this country," he added prophetically, as he sat cross-legged, looking ahead, held by the train of reflection.

After they had taken their rest, they proceeded with the journey. They saw the damage that was left by the protestors in the streets as well as contingents of police officers who were patrolling the city before they came up to Njoroge's charcoal yard in Bahati on the outskirts of the city.

"Waciuri, what happened? What took you so long since you left for Mula?" Njoroge asked as he greeted both of them.

And Waciuri told him of his decision to walk with the holy man rather than take the train. Njoroge updated them on the directions that political events had taken while he was away in Mula.

"Anyway, thank God you are fine. There are two Europeans prospecting for minerals in your village and a scout sent word that they were not sure of the intentions of those two foreigners. Someone should keep an eye on them," Njoroge said and gave Waciuri some pocket money after he told him of his intention to continue trekking to his village with Mohammed.

"Have it, you might need it on your journey," Njoroge told Waciuri as he bade them farewell the following day after hosting them for the night.

***

The rallies around the country were now becoming more organised as student leaders and civil society took over where PDA had left. They would move in a procession carrying placards and twigs, chanting and singing patriotic songs, as they loudly asked for change and the repeal of the law that had changed the country into a one party state.

Predictably, the police would come out with their batons and lob tear-gas at the crowds and a running battle would ensue. They would scatter, regroup, and move somewhere else to continue their rallies.

A week after Waciuri and Mohammed left the city, the situation was getting out of control as thousands of protestors took to the streets across the country in the largest show of defiance. It was as if the constant crackdowns had triggered a renewed strength in the masses.

In the city, thousands of people poured into the streets and most of them headed to Uhuru Square, where they converged and staged sit-in protests.

"Haki! yetu! Haki! yetu!" (Our! rights! Our! Rights!) one section of the crowd would chant, as another sectioned chanted, "Sonkoh! Must go! Sonkoh! Must go!" At some point, the crowd broke through a cordon formed by hundreds of riot police and Sonkoh's loyalists. With whips in hand, they stood helplessly watching. The

police became overwhelmed by the massive numbers even after calling for reinforcements.

Sonkoh and his coterie were watching the unfolding drama on prime time news with disbelief. They did not expect that the discontent that had started in a small way with a few disgruntled individuals in the country would get out of control. The crowds were not only asking for the repeal of the law that changed the country into a *de jure* one party state, but also had the audacity to say that he must go.

"Go where? Is this how they thank us after losing life and limb fighting for their independence?" President Sonkoh would ask his team.

Juma took that opportunity, when the government was under pressure from every quarter, to give press releases. And they were now coming at a constant frequency.

Juma accused the government of using its state machinery violently against its own civilians instead of addressing other pressing national issues like poverty and famine.

"The government of Sonkoh is neglecting the hungry and attempting to suppress information on the extent of the calamity. Instead, it is expending its energy in fighting its own citizens, whose only crime is asking for a better leadership," he would say.

"The famine in our country is a humanitarian crisis and yet the government is denying famine-related deaths. Instead, it is asking for proof. The president must accede to the will of the people and resign for negligence. Even the fish in the sea sometimes need a drink of water," he would add in his press statement.

Chapter Twenty Three

A week after Waciuri's grandfather was assaulted by the soldiers, his grandmother sat outside her compound. On the left of where she sat, was a fresh mound of red soil where her husband's grave stood.

Out of shock, she had not uttered a word since the death of her husband. Neighbours came to learn about the assault when they met her in the woods, fetching the bulbous leaves that were used to ease and treat bruises.

They consoled her, telling her that God does not sleep, that he was a witness to what had taken place in Mutituini village, and that he would right the wrongs that had been committed.

She was touched by their concern, more so because she knew that among them, some had also lost their loved ones in similar circumstances.

It was an evil that had been visited upon the quiet and sleepy village, like the plague that came with the white man in the early twentieth century. Those were awful times. People perished by the hundreds. Day by day, the disease would move from one hill to another, preceded by stories of the carnage it left on its way and how it resisted any known treatment. That was how Waciuri's grandmother would describe the atrocities that the government soldiers had committed if only she found the voice to do so.

Waciuri's grandmother would cook dinner and then heat the bulbous plants to treat her husband, who laid on a sleeping mat near the hearth to keep warm. Afterwards, she would make a bright fire burn in the hearth to keep him warm through the night.

But three days after the assault, Waciuri's grandfather succumbed despite all her efforts. It was in that kitchen, where the neighbours found her silently mourning the death of her husband.

She could not understand how death could snatch away her husband and leave her behind.

One week after Waciuri's grandfather's death, his grandmother passed on. After Waciuri's mother's demise, his grandmother was left with her husband and himself. Now that Waciuri had left for the city, she felt a big void in her life. And in any case, Waciuri's grandfather was the person she had spent most of her life with.

And just like old folks who have stayed married together for a long time, Waciuri's grandmother passed on peacefully in her sleep to join her husband on the other side.

"Where are you from?" one villager would ask another when they met on the village path.

"Haven't you heard? Waciuri has lost both grandparents and he is not even aware of it," the other villager would answer after coming from Waciuri's homestead where villagers had converged to make burial arrangements for the second time in a fortnight.

"The events are too tragic for words," the villager who had come from Waciuri's homestead would add, as they went their separate ways while shaking their heads and holding their chins in sorrow.

***

After watching live on TV the largest show of defiance since the uprising, the president held an urgent security meeting with his security chiefs.

"We cannot allow lawbreakers to run the country. Is the situation getting out of control?" the president asked those in the meeting.

"I would not say the situation is out of control, we have done our best with the little resources that we have," the police commissioner replied politely.

"Well! Your best is not good enough. Demonstrators have poured into areas that you were supposed to secure," the president told him.

"If we had enough vehicles to transport our men..." – "With all due respect to the commissioner, the situation is now beyond his control. What we need to do, is to contain the revolt decisively once and for all before it spins out of control," Ngei, the Minister for Defence and Home Affairs rudely cut out the police commissioner.

"I want this revolt dealt with forthwith. The damage has already been done and we cannot allow foreigners to tell us what to do. The country cannot be run on the whims of the populace."

And with that, tanks with machine guns mounted on them rolled into the city belching black diesel smoke, and accompanied by soldiers on armoured vehicles. They all moved towards Uhuru Square.

When they got to the square, some of the protestors laid prostrate on the ground, preventing the tanks from proceeding further. The rest of the tens of thousands of protestors chanted "Sonkoh! Must Go! *Haki! Yetu!*" And the commanding officer was at a loss on how to proceed.

He called his superiors for further instructions and the call was transferred to the red telephone line, the direct line to the president. After a brief consultation with Ngei and his inner circle of cabinet ministers, he instructed the soldiers to give the protestors twenty-four hours to leave the square in an orderly manner or else they would be removed by force.

"I've now engaged Emergency Laws to deal with the revolt, and if they defy, they will have to live with the consequences of that," the president told his coterie, who sat with him watching the unfolding live drama on TV.

With a count down looming, the standoff would continue to later in the day with demonstrators showing no signs of relenting. It was becoming obvious that, at some stage, the confrontation would develop into a violent encounter.

***

Since the head of the Special Branch sought permission from the president to bug the phone lines of those in the security committee and it was granted, the office and private lines of Ngei, the Minister for Defence and Home Affairs, had yielded some interesting leads.

From the conversations between Minister Ngei and MacClare, the Minister for Trade, his drinking buddy, it seemed that Minister Ngei could be letting some of the issues discussed in the security meeting out of the bag unwittingly when he had taken one too many.

They did not have hard evidence, and approaching Minister Ngei on the matter without disclosing how they had gathered the intelligence was out of the question. The only option was to gather enough intelligence and take the file to the president for further directions.

And when it seemed that they had gotten stuck in a *cul-de-sac*, an opportunity presented itself when the private line of Minister MacClare yielded a gold mine. In a telephone conversation with a yet to be known person, - even though spoken in coded language which they were able to decipher- MacClare had declared his misgivings about the two white foreigners who had gone to prospect for minerals in Mutituini village at the edge of Ol Donyokeri snow-capped mountain.

It was for that reason that Special Branch officers were trailing MacClare around the clock. They were observing him and gathering intelligence before finally bringing him in when the president gave his consent.

When the lights turned red at the roundabout near Uhuru Square, MacClare saw the cream Peugeot 504 that had been trailing him for some days a few metres behind him from his side mirror. He could see that the car was trying to squeeze out of the traffic jam in order to edge closer to him.

When the lights turned amber and because he had crossed the stop-line, he quickly stepped on the clutch, engaged the gear and released it before stepping on the accelerator, jerking the car forward before it gained momentum.

The sleuths were taken by surprise and, with the impunity that they were known for, they drew their guns and started driving on the incoming side of the road, pointing their guns on bemused drivers who moved out of their way to avoid a collision.

MacClare saw them from the right side of his front door's window as he was driving within the roundabout. He sped away as fast as he could towards the American Embassy.

In the meantime, the Peugeot had caused a traffic snarl-up which eventually blocked their vehicle. They came out of the car cursing and kicking the wheels in frustration.

They gave the description of the vehicle to traffic police manning the roads, with instructions to stop it and arrest its driver when they sight it, but with the chaos caused by demonstrators in town, it was going to be a tall order.

When MacClare got to the turn that led towards the American Embassy, he came across a police road block with a huge crowd milling around, shouting slogans.

Because the crowd was angry and was stoning cars, his car was waved by overwhelmed policemen to drive off quickly to avoid the ire of the crowd. And in the confusion, he was able to escape the dragnet that was set up to arrest him.

He would later learn that a school boy had been shot dead at the same spot when police officers attacked protestors with live bullets.

He eventually managed to drive to the embassy, where he sought protection after he gave them a detailed account of what led him there.

The government was utterly mortified when the international community learnt that it had sunk to such depths as to harass and try to arrest even its own cabinet ministers. The government was quickly losing its face in the eyes of the community of civilised nations.

Chapter Twenty Four

Waciuri and Mohammed were finally walking down the last ridge before they came to his village, and he was looking forward to getting home and meeting his grandparents and the people with whom he grew up.

It was a Saturday, the market day for Mutituini village, and by 11 a.m., the market was already crowded.

Villagers at the market centre are selling their vegetables and cereals while standing near their wares laid on the ground. Others are seated on roughly hewn benches under trees calling out for buyers. Traders are busy haggling on prices as they sell and buy. Most transactions are made in cash.

At the livestock yard, traders exchange lively banter and admire each other's herd as they wait for buyers.

Having trekked long distances, some of the weaker animals in the herd are already showing signs of fatigue. In one corner, a cow is lying on the ground, surrounded by others in the herd huddled under a tree.

"Look at the thin goat you are selling for the price of a cow, I will buy it at half the price you are selling," one buyer offers a seller who has tethered his goat with a rope tied to a wooden pin stuck into the ground.

"You know very well that the rains have failed us and it's by God's grace that this goat is still kicking. Do you now want me to give it to you a throw away price?" the seller replies.

"I'm afraid that is my final offer. If the rains failed, then that is not my fault," the buyer says.

"I'd rather go back home with my goat and slaughter it for my family than sell it to you at that price," the seller replies.

"Don't you think I know that you are a broker, who buys livestock at throw away prices in the village and then later sells them at exorbitant prices in the city?" the seller adds.

"Then take your goat to the city if you can and make those huge profits you want to make here," the buyer replies as he goes his way to try his luck somewhere else.

That is the kind of banter that you would find in the market, but on this particular market day, the banter lacked the spirit that the villagers of Mutituini were known for. It lacked enthusiasm.

When they finally got to the market, the commotion suddenly stopped. The market stood still as the villagers watched Waciuri and his friend make their way into the market; the tension in the air was so thick and pregnant with a sense of foreboding that you could have cut through it with a knife.

When he greeted them and made introductions, they seemed happy to have him back, but the welcoming energy that he knew the village possessed was not there.

It's as if a dark ominous cloud had descended on the quiet and idyllic place that was his village.

Later, his age mates told him of the tragedy that befell their village but omitted the part about what happened to his grandparents. They would leave that to Waciuri's neighbouring parents.

When later, neighbours he met on his way home insisted on him and his friend Mohammed taking tea at their homes even before they got to his homestead, he knew that something was wrong and enquired about it.

It was an elderly neighbour known for his ways with words and proverbs who finally broke the sad news to Waciuri.

Waciuri wore a brave face and insisted that he wanted to see the graves of his grandparents in their compound.

When he saw the two mounds of red soil marking the graves of his grandparents next to each other, as if death had fated them to lie close together, his chest heaved amid sobs. Tears freely streaked down his face onto the ground, making small holes on the dry red earth.

Mohammed held his shoulder to comfort him, and Waciuri in a flashback remembered the conversations and fables that his grandmother used to tell him. Now, with the strong woman, that was his grandmother, gone, he felt a profound loss, as if someone had ripped his soul apart.

After a few days of mourning and sojourn in his grandparents' homestead, Mohammed suggested that they go up the mountain to meditate and reflect as this would help him in healing his soul.

"Why do certain leaders cause so much pain and heartache to so many people instead of stepping down when required to do so?" Waciuri asked Mohammed as they walked towards the mountain.

"Man has always dominated his fellow man for his own benefit. And when he gets power, he uses it as a vehicle to do so. Power corrupts, and absolute power corrupts absolutely," he told him.

"Unfortunately, leaders in this part of the world think that they are chosen by God and it's only he who can decide when they should leave office and not the people who elected him," he went on.

"But why can't those people who surround him advise him when it becomes obvious that he has outlived his reign?" Waciuri asked in bewilderment.

"Those that surround the president are sycophants masquerading as advisors. They do not tell the president he is naked even when it is obvious that he is. If Sonkoh were to ask me who the bell tolls for, I would tell him not to ask for whom the bell tolls, for it tolls for you."

And they went on chatting until they came by the cabin where the two foreign prospectors had set base. They decided to find out what they were up to.

"I'm serving my Master who seeks to find the sacred river," Waciuri told the two white men as they made introductions.

They told him that they were prospecting for precious minerals, not before telling him that perhaps there was something wrong with his Master upstairs.

"Anyway, who would look for a big river on the mountain instead of looking in the low lands," the prospectors asked them.

"Perhaps you need a helping hand in your prospecting," Waciuri offered. "We have the instruments to help us and it's a bit technical for you people," one of the white men explained.

"You might need a pair of hands to help you with cooking and fetching water," Waciuri persisted.

"I think they would be useful in that aspect," the prospector who was talking to Waciuri sought the advice of his colleague.

They agreed and the two prospectors offered a small weekly stipend for their trouble. It wasn't much but Waciuri and Mohammed wanted to get to the bottom of this matter, if only to find out if they were in any way related to the deaths that had been visited upon his village.

If he found out that they were involved, he would feel that he had honoured his grandparents by exposing them to Juma and his gang who were holed up in the mountain.

***

On the same Saturday, back in the city, the chanting protestors wondered what fate awaited them as the standoff between them and the soldiers of the 4th

Armoured Battalion continued, like two fighting bulls that were sizing each other up, blowing their nostrils in rage.

The answer came on Sunday, when, after the twenty-four hours deadline had elapsed, Sonkoh's regime decided it had had enough.

The soldiers in the tanks began firing at the crowd just as they were ordered to do, causing a stampede. Those who had taken the bullets fell down.

In the most horrific day since the uprising began, the death toll began to climb after the shooting. By sunset that day, two hundred people lay dead from gunshot wounds. Others had succumbed after having been stampeded by those fleeing and scores more were injured.

Thousands of protestors shouting "We Want Freedom! Sonkoh! Must! Go!" chanted as they carried their slain comrades through the streets. Bystanders watched in disbelief.

"The regime has kidnapped the entire state and we want it back!" one protestor was heard saying.

As the day faded and lights flicked on across the city, the soldiers poured in across the suburbs.

The soldiers would go to peoples' homes, drag men and boys from their sleep, tell them to lie down on their stomachs in their compounds, and shoot them as they pleaded for mercy. All the while, other family members would watch and scream in horror.

The following day, the international community held a joint meeting to harshly condemn the brutal crackdown on the demonstrators.

"We condemn, in the harshest possible terms, the government's indiscriminate violence against its own people," the joint statement read.

A few days later, the ambassadors of Donyokeri in those countries were recalled. The UN Security Council decided to freeze the assets and foreign accounts of president Sonkoh, Ngei, the Minister for Defence and Home Affairs, Mr. Johnson, the AG, the president's kitchen cabinet and scores of other well connected businessmen who formed the cabal that surrounded the president.

A week after the senseless killings that took place in the capital city, Rukuna, the military split up into two factions. The brutal crackdown by the military against its own people was the final straw that broke the camel's back. It was the drop of water that made the pot run over.

A splinter group of the military made a statement from their base condemning the attack. It read in part, "The government has decided to respond with unprecedented brutality." It went on "The brutal crackdown has killed any vestiges of hope for a compromise and we call upon our brothers, our fellow soldiers, to join hands, end this tyrannical government and put in its place a democratic one."

Chapter Twenty Five

Waciuri and Mohammed had settled in quite well with the prospectors and Waciuri proved to be very useful to them.

He would go and fetch water from nearby streams for use in cooking and other daily chores. He would prove particularly useful in seeking goat milk which he bought from herders who took their mountain goats to the moorlands for grazing.

The milk particularly came in handy. They used it for making tea, which went a long way in helping to beat the cold harsh weather because of the proximity to the mountain.

The cabin housed a heavy metallic chest, which the prospectors claimed kept the instruments that were used to prospect. They claimed that they kept them locked because they were sensitive instruments that needed to be kept under lock and key.

On some days, the two foreigners would have a chart laid out in the open. They would pore over it as they scanned the area around them, talking in a foreign language that Waciuri did not comprehend.

"What language is it that those two speak among themselves," Waciuri asked Mohammed one day.

"They speak Russian and I have a hunch that those two are mercenaries," Mohammed told him.

"But time will tell, all in good time," he added as he went to perform his ritual morning prayers facing Mecca.

One day, Waciuri was sent to buy goat liver and prepare a steamy meal using local herbs. The treat was for a visitor who was arriving that afternoon.

It had to be a special visitor because the prospectors

had taken out and placed on the dining table a bottle of Red Label vodka, to accompany the lunch.

That afternoon, Singh, a burly Indian who wore a black turban on his head, came visiting and was received outside by the white men before they proceeded into the cabin to have lunch.

"I wonder who that visitor is," Waciuri asked Mohammed as they sat outside the cabin having their own lunch.

"I wonder too, all in good time my son. All in good time," Mohammed replied. They could hear the noisy banter of the prospectors and the visitor inside the cabin.

"How did you come to meet those two anyway?" the burly Indian whispered to his hosts as they sat drinking the vodka after having taken their lunch. They told him how they met.

"Do you think that is a coincidence?" Singh asked as he exhaled smoke from the cigar that he was offered, filling the room with a cloudy grey smoke creating doughnut rings that rose up lazily to the ceiling of the cabin.

They told him that they were ignorant people and would not be able to discern what they were up to. They even told Singh that they thought the old man was a nut case.

"I will take no chances with them; I'll have to do my own investigations," the ever suspicious Singh told them. He burst out of the door to look for Waciuri.

Singh was a police reservist working for the Special Branch and had been sent there after they got the intel from the intercepted phone conversation between the now fugitive MacClare and a yet to be identified person.

"Young man, who sent you here!" Singh barked at Waciuri. "No one, we came looking for a job before proceeding with our journey," Waciuri replied, putting on a brave face as he said so.

"Master indeed! We shall see about that," Singh snarled at him. He held him by the collar of his shirt and dragged him towards the mountain.

"I will throw you down a cliff if you don't confess and tell me who sent you here. Your real masters that is," Singh told him as he frog marched him towards the mountain side.

The other two white mercenaries had meanwhile taken Mohammed into their custody to see if they could get some truth from him.

The two mercenaries had been brought to the country by Sonkoh and his security team to prop up the soldiers in one final assault on the rebels hiding in the mountain. They would bring their vast war experience, which they got by fighting wars as dogs-of-war in the Congo, Equatorial Guinea and other African countries under the tutelage of the notorious Bob Denard.

As one former French foreign minister once said, "Africa is the only continent where France can still change the course of history with a few hundred men." Apparently, president Sonkoh and his team had taken that statement literally.

***

After the splinter group from the military made their announcement, they were now heading to the city, but not before meeting stiff resistance from the other half consisting of loyal soldiers. The only advantage was that the dissident soldiers were from the armoured division and had more tanks than the others.

The only game changer was the Air Force, which had not yet made their stand on where their allegiance stood. The UN Security Council had been unable to enforce a no-fly-zone over Donyokeri because The Soviet Union and China were opposed to it.

The rebel army had met little resistance as it made its way towards the city after consolidating other major towns, but had met heavy resistance from loyalist troops as they neared the city. They held them back with sustained blasts from rocket-fire, mortars and anti-aircraft guns. This also made it impossible for their small light planes to make reconnaissance missions.

The loyal soldiers had also booby-trapped the roads with mines, making the rebel advance slow down.

The rebel soldiers, under the stewardship of Major General Akilimali, came up with a plan of attacking the city from three different flanks. The idea was to put pressure on the loyalists on three different fronts and eventually trap them in, leaving no room for escape.

And it seemed to work because they were now inching towards the capital amid stiff resistance from loyalist and foreign fighters.

"This battle is not going well, why haven't you scrambled jets to blasts out the approaching tanks as I had instructed earlier? That would have staved off the rebellion before it got to this stage," president Sonkoh asked his Defence Minister as they strategized from the safety of State House. His confident and loud voice was noticeably missing as he spoke.

"There was some disquiet in the Air Force when some soldiers refused to take orders, but they have been court marshaled and executed for defying their superior commanders," Ngei, the Minister for Defence and Home Affairs, assured him.

"In fact as we speak, the jets are refueling before going for their mission of dropping bombs on the advancing rebels," he added.

There was an uncomfortable silence in the room as they wondered when this rebellion was going to be contained and those officers who had rebelled court marshaled.

Other than his wife and kitchen cabinet, he had also instructed the Governor of the Central Bank to drop by just in case. He had reminded him not to forget to carry two briefcases full of crisp 100 American dollar bills.

He had also instructed his loyal pilot to stand by at Sandton Airport. In fact, the pilot was given a hefty daily allowance to stay at the airport away from his family awaiting further instructions. And he made use of the idle time drinking cognac and entertaining different women.

The Governor of the Central Bank had meanwhile taken three briefcases full of American dollars and instructed his accounting officers to debit the president who had asked for a small loan. He kept the other briefcase to himself saying under his breath "you never know how things will turn out."

Chapter Twenty Six

Juma's scouts had been watching for some time the two foreigners who had built a cabin near the fringes of the mountain.

On this particular day, they saw a burly Indian holding a boy by the collar of his shirt, leading him towards a cliff on the mountain.

As usual, they had been instructed to report any unusual activities near the mountain to avoid a surprise attack and they thought this was one they should report to their commander, Juma.

They immediately called him using the walkie-talkies that they were given, and Juma told them he was on his way.

Singh meanwhile had tied a rope around Waciuri's hip and had managed to lower him onto the face of the cliff. Waciuri gave him a spirited resistance, and he had to acknowledge that the boy had given him a hard time, despite his age, but obviously could not match his strength.

He had tied the other end of the rope to a metal hook stuck into the ground and held a penknife with which he would cut the rope once he got the information he wanted.

"I'm giving you the final chance, you either tell me who sent you to spy on those two or I cut the rope sending you cascading down the cliff to the rocky bottom," Singh barked at Waciuri, who was now trying to cling precariously with his fingers and feet on the protruding rocks on the face of the cliff.

"Please hic! Pull me hic! Up. I'm going to cooperate. I'm not able to talk in this situation," Waciuri replied back incoherently amid wails.

"I can't hear you, you fool! Speak up! I don't have all da..."- he was interrupted when, Juma, who had crept stealthily behind him, hit his head with his rifle butt, cracking his skull and sending him flying down the cliff.

Bildad meanwhile was heaving Waciuri up the cliff using the rope. The boy tearfully hugged both of them when they finally hauled him up.

He was especially happy to be reunited with Juma, but then remembered he had left behind Mohammed and did not know what fate had befallen him.

"Please! Please, I left my Master back at the cabin with two mercenaries and I don't know their fate," Waciuri told them with a worried look on his face.

They crept to the cabin and peered through the window. Mohammed, who was badly beaten and had his hands tied up with a cord, was lying on the cold floor wincing in pain.

"This fool is either telling the truth or he is too good with secrets," one of the mercenaries told his comrade.

"I wonder what has taken Singh so long, perhaps he should come and tell us what to do with him," the other told him.

"Ah! There he is, speak of the devil...." the other mercenary said as he went to open the door after they heard a knock on the door.

When he opened the door, he was met with two men pointing AK 47 rifles at him. "Pull back and don't try any monkey tricks," Juma snarled at the mercenary as they stormed their way through the door. Waciuri was left behind in case of a shoot-out.

The other mercenary was caught by surprise and did not have time to draw his Beretta M9 pistol from the back of his hip. The weapon was held in place by his trouser.

"We know who you are, and anyway forget about your

Indian friend, he had an appointment with his maker," Juma told the surprised men.

"You can't shoot us unless you want the soldiers in the nearby camp to come for you when they hear the gunshots," one of them said defiantly with a sneer on his face after they had been ordered to kneel down.

"We don't intend to waste our bullets on you two," Juma replied him and, as if on cue, he and Bildad hit both men with their rifle butts on their heads, sending them sprawling down on the floor.

They carried the badly injured Mohammed, who was barely speaking, outside, where Waciuri stood with a gourd of cold mountain spring water that he intended to give him.

When Mohammed saw Waciuri, he broke into a strained smile with tears on his face, He now saw that his young friend was alive and well.

Waciuri helped his Master take the water from the gourd as Juma held his head to prop him up into a sitting position. He drank the water in dainty sips.

"You know" Mohammed labourously said as he let out a painful cough that came from his chest. "I've lived in this world for a considerably long time and have never met a true friend like you."

"Me neither, I've learnt a lot from you which no school would have ever taught me," Waciuri replied. "But remember what I told you; seek to expand your mental horizons, even if it means losing sight of the shore in search of your purpose," Mohammed said in between chesty coughs.

"Don't talk like that," Waciuri said with a tinge of alarm in his voice. Juma and Bildad followed the conversation quietly.

"I've been on the mountain top, and have looked over, and I have seen the Promised Land of your country's second liberation. I may not get there with you, but you my son, will get there," Mohammed continued. Now Waciuri was really getting concerned.

And then, Mohammed saw it and cried out "there! Look! The Sacred River!" With a strength that baffled everyone, he rose to walk as Waciuri tried to restrain him.

"Don't strain yourself," Waciuri told him, trying to hold him but was held back by Juma and Bildad.

He walked limping towards the snow-capped Ol Donyokeri Mountain. In the distance, amid the glaring light, he saw it! The Stream of Life, as clear as crystal, flowing from the mountain. On each side of the river stood trees of different types that had bloomed, producing an array of colourful flowers.

The stream was sparkling from the glorious light and was crystal clear, such that, he could see the gold and tiger fish that swam gracefully at the bottom on its bed.

In the middle of the river, stood the great *Mugumo* tree, whose figs had sprouted. The figs of the tree were for the healing of nations.

There would be no more death, neither mourning, nor crying or pain, for the former things had passed.

Then he heard a glorious voice saying, "to him who is thirsty I will give to drink without cost from the spring of life. He who overcomes will inherit all this. You, my servant, you have overcome, you may drink from it!" and he fell down to drink...

"What is happening," Waciuri worriedly asked when he saw Mohammed fall on the rocky ground of the mountain's moorland. His mind was floating, thinking perhaps it was all a bad dream.

"He was hallucinating, but he has now passed on," Juma told Waciuri who was now crying uncontrollably. And both Juma and Bildad placed their hands on his heaving shoulders.

He was so distraught that for once he thought that if he had been given a choice, he would have chosen never to be born. He would never wish this bittersweet existence unto anyone. Not after losing two of his best confidants; his grandmother, and Mohammed in such a short span of time.

Then they heard a shriek of noise from afar. The noise drew closer. They heard women ululating in triumph and spontaneous cries of joy.

They looked perplexed at each other until someone came running to inform them that the soldiers had made a hasty retreat to go back to the city to support the loyalist soldiers, who were now losing the battle to the rebel soldiers.

Juma called Muthoni with his walkie-talkie and told her to come down the forest with the rest of the group and prepare to head to the city. They also made arrangements with the Imam of that location and other Muslims to perform the burial rites on the departed Mohammed.

***

That cloudy grey, Wednesday, the rebels were within less than fifty kms of Rukuna, the capital city of Donyokeri, and the loyalists and hired foreign fighters were putting up a spirited resistance.

Sustained blasts from rocket fire and mortars rang out the whole day from both sides, sending civilians to the safety of their homes as they anxiously wondered what would happen in the next few days. They were uncertain of what hand the future held for them.

People were not going to work to avoid being caught up in the crossfire and food stocks had ran dangerously low in their homes. Other desperate and daring civilians risked their lives by venturing out to loot closed businesses but at a heavy price. Those caught looting were shot on sight as the country was now under Emergency Laws.

But sometimes even the fear of being shot dead could not overcome the pangs of hunger. Of course, there were those opportunists who took advantage of the situation to loot electronic appliances and other high end goods that they had always dreamt of owning, gleefully carrying the most that they could with their hands. Some even used *mkokoteni* (carts) to cart away stolen goods.

At noon, the state television, which was most of the time playing patriotic songs and intermittently announcing state propaganda, caught people's attention. The president was about to make an announcement.

"Dear country-men and women of this beloved country. I greet you. The situation is under control, and we ask those misguided youths fighting the people's government, which you elected, to lay down their arms. It is not too late to negotiate. We shall not seek retribution if they lay down their arms..." the president said to the people. One could not help but notice his tomato red eyes. Even the eye drops that he had earlier applied did not help to conceal his weary, fearful eyes.

He was now really counting on the fighter jets to obliterate the advancing tanks. This would change the battle theater completely.

One hour later, after the president had made his address on state television, Major General Akilimali made his through the radio and told the cornered president that it was too little too late to negotiate. His olive branch was a ruse meant to hoodwink them because the president's ruthlessness preceded him.

Meanwhile, the scrambled jets laden with missiles were now airborne and would reach their targets in twenty minutes.

***

Juma was joined by his group after the surrounding forest disgorged the men it had swallowed up. They stood at the cabin waiting for Bildad's turquoise coloured Bedford lorry that would ferry them to Rukuna to join the splinter army rebel group under the command of Major General Akilimali.

"Can I join you? Especially now that I have no one left in my family here in the village," Waciuri pleaded with Juma.

"Well, if you have to come to the city with us, then I'll need to find you accommodation," Juma replied.

"It's not safe for you to be with us at the frontline, but I promise if we come out of this, I'll see you through college. You are like a small brother to me," he went on to reassure him.

Earlier, while waiting for his gang, Juma had shot open the padlock that hid the contents inside the metallic chest to reveal an assortment of weapons.

Inside the chest, were rifles with telescopic lenses, Taurus pistols, grenades and night vision goggles, among other items. He wondered aloud how all those were meant to be used against them.

The lorry finally came, and there was no time to waste. They loaded their weapons together with the others retrieved from the chest and drove towards the city, only stopping briefly at Mutituini market to acknowledge wild cheers from their fellow villagers.

It would take less time than it normally took to drive from Mutituini to Rukuna as there were few vehicles on the road owing to the situation in the country.

Chapter Twenty Seven

The tanks were now on the radar sights of the jet fighters. The drivers had scampered away from them when they heard the splitting roar of the approaching jets.

To their surprise, the jets did a fly past, but not before twisting round and round and flying off to a neighbouring country where the young pilots hoped to be offered political asylum after their defection.

They had agreed to fly the jets for the mission to avoid being summarily executed had they refused. In actual fact, they had chosen to stand in solidarity with their fellow rebel soldiers.

The soldiers on the ground broke into a cheer and clapped when they realised that the pilots had spinned their jets as a sign of solidarity with their cause.

And now the president knew that his goose was cooked. He contemplated an exit plan incase his loyal soldiers failed to retake control of the country.

He was now seriously thinking about cutting his losses and fleeing, especially after the constant anxious pleas of the first lady Marie became unbearable.

"My dear, isn't it about time we left the country? God knows what those rascals would do to you if they took us in their custody," his wife would remind him as she applied a face mask, sitting across a table mirror beside the bed. Actually, she was saying so to save her skin not as much as his.

President Sonkoh looked at her face with the white face mask she had applied it on. The mask made her look like a witch doctor, and he wondered whether what scared him most was getting caught by the rebels or staring at her.

"Don't worry my queen; I have secured a safe haven from the president of our neighbouring country. In fact he is wondering what I'm still doing here," Sonkoh exasperatedly replied to sooth her fears. When he took the bride price to her parents back in the days, she was then a beautiful maiden to behold, not what she had turned out to be.

Marie, the first lady, was an extravagant, vain woman who wore too much jewellery on her neck. It made her look like she was sagging forward from their weight, and her once beautiful face now looked ashen from the many make-up types that she experimented with. She also had a short temper that her workers had learnt to live with.

Her frequent foreign trips to shop for expensive designer wear and perfumes were unmatched. It gave her a kick when she did so. In fact, people who knew about her shopping habits whispered to themselves that she was not only the first lady, but also the first shopper.

***

Juma and his gang finally made contact with Major General Akilimali and were warmly welcomed to their ranks. The soldiers could do with all the help that came their way.

After the rebel soldiers had begun their uprising, militia men with the help of rebel soldiers were manning the roads by putting up make shift roadblocks using logs spiked with jutting nails. They would also stop vehicles and inspect them to see if they were transporting loyalists.

The roadblocks proved to be very useful in stalling the soldiers who had been recalled back to the city from the mountains and forests where they had gone to fight the PDA activists. Some of the soldiers had defected to the opposition side when they realised that the loyalists were losing ground in the city. It was a matter of self preservation.

When drivers of the few civilian cars on the road were flagged down for inspection, they would come out and shout "Power! Power!" in solidarity with the rebels. After thorough inspection of the vehicles, they would be flagged off to proceed with their journey.

These are the kind of road blocks that Juma and his group encountered on their way to the city. And whenever the militia realised who he was, they saluted him, encouraging him to fight on for the cause. They acknowledged that he and other like - minded members of PDA were the ones who triggered the uprising.

They also found out that he was the one who released press statements to the media from his hideout in the forest and thereby made the world aware of the atrocities that president Sonkoh's soldiers had committed in the villages.

The following day, rebel soldiers were now fifteen kms from the city. Earlier that day, explosions and gunfire rocked the city, with rebel leader Major General Akilimali and Juma making a joint statement insisting the end for Sonkoh was near.

A defiant and apparently isolated Sonkoh urged his followers to fight the rebels to defend their country from colonial masters and their agents.

The road that led to the city was strewn with hundreds of dead fighters from both sides and carcasses of burnt out tanks and armoured vehicles lay scattered everywhere.

Later that day, Sonkoh said he would not surrender and pledged to emerge victorious. "We'll not; we'll not abandon Rukuna to rebels and their imperialist agents," he declared.

On the other hand, the rebel leaders made their own statements urging the president to surrender to stop further bloodshed.

"The desperate statements of President Sonkoh are kicks of a dying horse," Major General Akilimali had said when he informed international reporters that they were working on an interim council to oversee a post-Sonkoh government and a road map to the future.

Juma on his part had urged the president to hand over power and accept defeat. "Sonkoh is a drowning man latching onto a straw, that's what he is doing," he had addressed a battery of reporters thus.

"Silence never won any rights. They are not handed down from above, they are forced by pressures from below," he would add.

That night, the fighting wore on with blasts ringing the whole night and illuminating the dark like fireworks while the lights of the city flickered intermittently.

The following day was a cold morning and the fighting had now entered the city. Rebels pushed to consolidate the city as they exchanged heavy fire with Sonkoh's presidential guards and snipers on top of tall buildings.

The presidential guards were the *crème de la crème* of the military and proved their mettle in holding their ground. The snipers had also made the advance of the rebels difficult and slow and the battle dragged on to late that afternoon.

It was becoming a difficult urban warfare that would give Sonkoh ample time to escape, something which the rebels were desperately trying to stop. Suddenly, a heavy fog that had never been witnessed in the recent history of Donyokeri descended on the city like a heavy blanket.

How Weather Has Contributed to Change the Course of History

In 1815, in the Battle of Waterloo, Napoleon was defeated by the British because of extreme weather conditions.

This development, in turn, played a key role in the rise of the British Empire. But in recent history, the most important event where weather has played a decisive impact on world shaking events is the Battle of Stalingrad.

Operation Barbarossa was the code name for German's invasion of the Soviet Union. It was the largest military operation in human history in terms of both manpower and casualties.

For example, by mid 1942, the German invasion had already cost Russia over six million soldiers.

By the spring of 1942, despite the failure of Operation Barbarossa to defeat the Soviet Union in a single campaign, the war had been progressing well for the Germans.

The German offensive to capture Stalingrad, which commenced in the late summer of 1942 was supported by intensive Luftwaffe bombing which reduced much of the city to rubble.

And with the Germans controlling over ninety percent of the city at times, the Soviet defenders were barely clinging on tenaciously.

Then it happened! In November 1942, the Russian (Arctic) winter set in and the German sixth Army weakened rapidly from cold, starvation and ongoing Soviet resistance.

Coupled with the failure of re-supply by air, by early 1943, the battle of Stalingrad was lost and the remaining surrounded sixth Army surrendered.

The battle of Stalingrad was lost. Had Hitler

*defeated the Soviet Union, the course of history as
we know it today would be very different.*

The rebels took advantage of the fog to pound the city
blocks with artillery fire where the presidential guards
and snipers had taken positions. They moved blindly to
consolidate control of the entire city and its environs. It
was a suicidal move, but they chose to take it.

Then as mysteriously as the fog had appeared, it
disappeared, revealing a gorgeous glow of the setting
sun.

Earlier that cold afternoon, president Sonkoh was
holed up at State House with members of his kitchen
cabinet and the governor of the Central Bank, engaged
in a heated argument.

"You should at least ensure a safe exit for those of us
who are here," Mr. Johnson, the AG proffered.

"It is beyond my call now my friends, it's everyone for
himself and God for us all," president Sonkoh told them
resignedly.

"What now, are you chickening out and abdicating
your duty as the commander-in-chief of the armed
forces?" a furious Ngei, the Minister for Defence and
Home Affairs, barked at the president when they
apparently saw the first lady hauling a large heavy
luggage across the corridors of power.

"What about those of us who have stood by you?"
he added. "Well, we have a saying in my community,
that even when your own house is burning, you should
at least warm yourself with its heat," the president
philosophically said as he ordered his bodyguards to see
him through to the parking bay.

The Governor was engrossed in his own thoughts
amid the din, as he thought about the wise decision he
took of stashing away some money for himself. At least,
that would take care of him and his family. He had also

been careful to make arrangements for them to leave the country.

The presidential armoured car, with headlights on because of zero-visibility, was now racing towards Sandton airport where his trusted pilot was waiting for him.

The rebels wanted to seal all exits, and a number of jeeps were also racing towards Sandton airport for that reason. They had strict instructions to put him into their custody alive so that he could face charges of mismanaging the country and stifling democracy.

Finally, the president got to the airport and boarded the waiting Cessna light aircraft that stood on the tarmac, with his wife in tow dragging the heavy luggage that had her jewellery and assorted designer wear. Earlier on, she had broken a heel of one of her stilettos when she tripped, which made her limp along grotesquely.

The pilot had to wait a bit for the fog to clear before he started careening away as the plane gained speed. It was the longest wait for Sonkoh. Just then, the pilot saw two jeeps blocking the aircraft's path far ahead and informed the president accordingly.

"Just keep on going you ignoramus! There's enough distance to take off," the president barked at his pilot.

"Then we have to drop off some luggage to lift off," the pilot responded. "Throw over your luggage onto the tarmac!" the president spat out, with his brow all furrowed, at Marie. She hesitated and clung to it tightly, like a sulky juvenile.

When she saw the fiery red eyes of her husband, she reluctantly threw the luggage onto the tarmac before Sonkoh thought of tossing her out herself as excess luggage. She knew what her husband was capable of.

The Cessna started lifting off gradually, as it approached the parked jeeps in front of its path, and the rebel soldiers jumped out in panic and scampered away.

The nose of the aircraft was lifting up in the air and the sight of the jeeps was now receding below.

"Forget about the luggage dear, we can always buy those again. I have kept a little fortune in the Cayman Islands," Sonkoh told his wife reassuringly. He let out a sigh of relief.

"I told you I had taken care of business and there was no need to worry," he added as the plane lifted itself above the jeeps.

***

...the fog disappeared mysteriously as fast as it had appeared revealing the gorgeous glow of the sunset. Rebel forces had overran the city after loyalists troops had fled.

And after news of the takeover of the city by the rebels finally came out, thousands poured out into the streets that evening to celebrate. Civilians were elatedly shouting "Power to the people!"

"Sonkoh must pay!" those who drove to the city centre chanted and honked their car horns incessantly in celebration.

The crowds had portraits of the president and his effigy. They converged at Uhuru Square where they lit the portraits and stepped on them, baying for his blood. One person in the deliriously excited crowd took a rope and made a noose around the head of Sonkoh's effigy.

As the day faded and lights flickered on across the city, another person in the jubilant crowd addressed journalists. She talked loudly, no longer afraid in a country where political opinions had always been whispered.

Meanwhile, Major General Akilimali and his rebel

forces, accompanied by Juma and his band, raided and overran the fortified State House in heavy fighting to flush out the remnants of Sonkoh's loyalists who were still holed up in the building.

A BBC correspondent who had accompanied them said, "the rebels have breached the compound and entered inside. They have taken State House completely. It's over!"

Inside, they found Ngei, the Minister for Defence and Home Affairs; Mr. Johnson the AG; and the Central Bank Governor, among others, who made up the inner circle that surrounded Sonkoh and who had ruled the country through proxy for many years.

They would be charged with political mismanagement of the country, crimes against humanity and economic crimes. Their homes and offices were later searched and their passports and those of their family members confiscated to ensure they didn't leave the country. A briefcase full of American dollars was found in the Central Bank governor's bedroom safe and would be used as exhibit number 1 in his trial for economic crimes against the state.

Inside State House, it was agreed that Major General Akilimali would address journalists during the announcement of a joint statement. Among those who flanked the battle-hardened soldier leader were Juma, Bildad and Muthoni.

He said that the rebel soldiers would initially take control of the country for the first six months to stabilize it. This would allow the country prepare for a referendum to find out if it was ready for a new constitution that would herald a new dawn in the hands of a new and better leadership.

He also made a directive to the police to have all political prisoners held under the instructions of the deposed government to be released forthwith.

And the whole world, among them Donyokerians, saw and heard the address in the evening's special bulletin news. Among those who witnessed the historic announcement was Mumbi, who sat having a dinner with her other relatives in their home in Rukuna.

And there she sat, in the sitting room in a house in the city in a country on the continent in the world, - watching the live drama.

She almost choked on her food when she saw the image of Juma sitting pensively as Major General Akilimali addressed the nation. She did not follow the rest of the speech and the battery of questions that the journalists shot at them. She sat glued to Juma's image that flickered on the screen. A childish glow filled her and warmed her heart. Tomorrow she would go looking for her beloved one.

Meanwhile, thousands of people continued pouring into the streets of the city in celebrations and festivities that would continue for many days to come.

***

As the nose of the aircraft was lifting up in the air and the sight of the jeeps was receding down below, suddenly, the folding wheels hit the windshield of one of the jeeps. The jeep tore through the underside of the plane, making it to lose balance. It came down on the hard tarmac.

The plane careened on the runway in a zigzag manner as the fuselage slid on the tarmac, producing red sparks before, without warning, it burst into a ball of flames that quickly engulfed the whole plane.

Those inside the plane screamed in terror. They sat trapped inside as the relenting tongues of flames consumed them. By the time a fire extinguisher truck was dispatched to the burning plane to contain the fire, those inside had been burnt beyond recognition.

The following morning, Mumbi waded through the sea of reporters and people who had milled the entrance of the Inter Continental Hotel, now used as a press centre. She found Juma and his team fielding questions.

"I'll take no more questions, you have to appreciate we haven't slept a wink since yesterday's events," Juma tried to wind up the interview.

"Excuse me!" one journalist cut him short. And when he was about to talk, Juma saw Mumbi amid the crowd, jostling in the stifling hot room. He excused himself as he went to meet her.

Juma gave her a bear hug in her now opened arms and a smile creased his face after the long lingering hug. She poked his face and asked "Juma! Is that you Juma?" she vividly remembered the day they kissed and held hands near the waterfall back in the village. They both wished then, that the day would never end.

Waciuri, who was also there, was not left behind as he embraced his long time friend Mumbi. He considered her the big sister that he never had. As tears of joy streamed down her face, she could not help but notice that Juma had grown sagely old, like one who had seen a lot in his young life.

PART THREE

Early Eighties

Chapter Twenty Eight

It had been ten years since Sonkoh's government had been deposed and nine years since a referendum has been held, pitting the old constitution that was handed over by the British against the new one that was drafted by the Committee of Experts.

The people had chosen the latter. It greatly curtailed the enormous powers of the president that was entrenched in the former constitution. It also had decentralised power from the capital city and spread it to the counties by the creation of a devolved government.

Citizens would now make decisions on how the funds that were generated in their county were going to be best utilised to develop their own counties, which would be run by a Governor elected by them.

After the new constitution was adopted, a general election was held soon after to elect the next government, and Juma sailed through as the new president owing to his role in the struggle for the second liberation of the country. His heroics had made him popular and visible throughout the country.

In his inauguration speech at Uhuru Square, where a sea of thousands of people had come to witness as he took the oath of office, he had addressed the multitude of people thus:

"A new dawn has come to our beloved country. We brought to life a dream that had wafted too long. We broke a storm that had raged more than humanely bearable. We realised a vision held back for decades by all sort of malevolent forces.

The constitution has also raised the bar of leadership, offering the country a platform upon which to anchor new standards that expect nothing but the very best of those who seek to manage our public affairs."

Not very long afterwards, he had married his sweetheart Mumbi in an elaborate wedding that was attended by dignitaries from around the world. Bildad stood as his best man and Muthoni was the best maid. She was a friend to Juma and had fought beside him in the forest. She had also taught Mumbi at Jamhuri Secondary School and Mumbi did not see why she couldn't be her best maid.

Mumbi's father, Kamangu, knew that he would not be elected to any government post in the general elections owing to his past experience with the villagers of Mutituini, and so he opted to direct his energies to his farm. He also did not attend his daughter's wedding to Juma as he did not approve of him; he had not reconciled himself to the fact that Juma had played a key role in the events that had taken place in the country.

Bildad had replaced MacClare as the Minister of Trade owing to his entreprenual skills. He would apply these to oversee the indigenization of business ownership and ensure they met international best standards of business practices to make them competitive.

Immediately after the change of guard, Muthoni had gone to the US to pursue a degree in law. She had always wanted to practice law after her parents were killed and they lost their land when they were falsely accused of being freedom fighters during the colonial period by their neighbours, who were then Home Guards. She would seek to ensure that no one would go through an injustice like the one she went through.

When she came back after four years, she opened a law practice for women and the less priviledged in the society. After practicing for five years, she was appointed to head the Human Rights Commission in the country. She was still a spinster.

MacClare was elevated to the Ministry of Defence and Home Affairs owing to his contribution to the struggle for the second liberation of the country.

Otieno, a leader of PDA who had been released after the amnesty to release all political prisoners in the country, became the Inspector-General of the National Police Service. He was appointed by president Juma after he was approved by parliament.

He oversaw the disbanding of the dreaded Special Branch and oversaw the establishment of the National Intelligence Service in accordance with the new constitution.

He ensured that it was a professional body that would be responsible for gathering intelligence without ever using torture to extract information.

By doing so, he felt that he had honoured his father who had died while he was incarcerated at the State Research Bureau. He also ensured that Opiyo and other torturers of the notorious Special Branch faced justice for their crimes.

Waciuri never forgot the last words of his friend Mohammed, to expand his mental horizons even if it meant losing sight of the shore to discover new lands. And most importantly, to find out the purpose that destiny had prepared for him.

After what he had gone through, he knew that without a doubt, destiny had prepared him to serve his people back in the village.

And for that reason, when he cleared high school, he requested his friend from back then, president Juma, to facilitate his studies abroad. With his wish granted after President Juma kept his promise, Waciuri went ahead to study Political Science and Philosophy in Germany.

When he came back after further studies, he went to his village and took the position of advisor to the government, for which he had applied earlier.

It was just like he had left it - idyllic and sleepy with undulating rolling hills that were covered with a lush green carpet of vegetation.

It was always good to be home, he thought as he smelt the fresh air of the countryside. When he got to his grandparents' homestead, it was tended to. The neighbours had ensured that it was not overgrown with weeds as their son went to gain knowledge in faraway lands and bring that knowledge home. Only a few dry leaves that had fallen from the mango tree where chickens used to perch broke the monotonous tidiness.

When neighbours saw him coming, they ululated and broke out in spontaneous cries of joy as they welcomed their son back home. That day, a large he-goat was unlucky and kegs of *muratina* (local beer) went around. They sat outside that night snuggled around a bonfire, talking and reminiscing about the past.

He soon thereafter left for the city where he worked briefly as an advisor to the government and made a name for himself in the political circles.

He also made money, and used to while most evenings at the Princess Hotel. That is where he met his future wife, Virginia Chebet, a doctor, whose parents, Wambui and Bundotich, had been active in the struggle for independence as freedom fighters.

Paying bride price for his wife had been an elaborate affair. He asked Bildad to be his right-hand man in the negotiations.

In such negotiations, he could not address the in-laws of his future wife directly and thus the need for someone to negotiate on his behalf.

The other important role that the right-hand man played was to try and haggle the bride price downwards as much as possible using wit and proverbs to do so, and Bildad proved quiet capable in that task.

However, it proved costly in other ways, like on every occasion they met, they had to carry five kegs of *muratina* and the many in-laws were entitled to something from them.

But eventually, they went through the formal negotiations and Bundotich finally gave her daughter's hand in marriage.

Waciuri's itching desire to serve his people at the grassroots continued to burn in him, and after two years, he resigned his government post to vie for the elective post of governor for his county, which he won with a landslide.

He oversaw a rapid development of the county through his pragmatic and honest leadership.

With his foresight, rather than stick to peasant farming, he had shifted the county from agriculture to industry by inviting investors and using the devolved funds to build eighty factories, ranging from manufacturing and, textiles to steel and real estate.

With his stewardship, most families lived in a modern house and each family was entitled to free education for their children and health care. In addition to the salaries that they earned from working in the factories, every worker was entitled to dividends.

It was a phenomenal economic transformation for a community that, just ten years ago, had villagers struggle to save from their farm proceeds to buy a bicycle.

Gradually, as the sun set, dipping into the darkness below the horizon to be reborn the next morning as a young and glowing god, the shrill of millions and millions of insects punctuated the still night of Mutituini village. The villagers slept assured of a brighter future.

"Hold fast to dreams, for if dreams die,
Life is a broken-winged bird
That cannot fly."

Langstone Hughes (1902-1967)

American Writer, Essayist and Poet